Believe My Eyes

I was playing with the children until I heard you come in through the door, whispering to be quiet because I'm here when you came with him and I felt grim. I can't shake off the feeling of green envy and jealousy. I acted like I didn't care and looked away, pretending not to see. I'm jamming alone to music that makes me think of you and thinking what we could be. I'm pretending I'm fine as I sit and lay back on this tree and watch the forest spirits dance away. I sit and wonder why and how this could be and to what degree I must endure this, keeping the feelings at bay. I plug in the headphones and sway to the music, pretending we're in a music video where I'm teaching you Spanish as you cook the pescatarian food on a sunny day. You play with my hair and fix it, giggling at how messed up it is as I stare into your hazel eyes. I rationalized things away as you chased down the halls looking for me, wanting to return something I left but I wasn't there. I think I need some therapy because I'm crazy. I remember calling you adorable for such an act but you know we make the perfect pair, the perfect team against the world that isn't fair. We won't wear and tear because behind the stern faces we're bubbly and child-like even if we love to swear. I stare at the blue moon and pretend I bought you the over priced gift just to see your reaction of disbelief turned to loving expressions that you only say with your eyes. It goes beyond the contract but this one subtraction can cause friction between us and even though it can be a distraction, I'd like to pretend we have an attraction. I pretend you tell me that you like me, too, and I try to keep my cool but I can't as I exclaim in joy how I haven't felt butterflies in such a long time and can put this into action. Awakened by the rain, I slump my hands into my pockets with a cigarette in my mouth and walk home to daydream a wonderful interaction between us. A temporary set back, insane as it sounds, there might be something there and I'm willing to work on it. Strategizing during my time off as you're stuck on my mind wishing I didn't feel just a little bit. Maybe you'll give me another warm smile by the time of my arrival and perhaps I'll be your favorite. I blink away and have to keep this boy next door persona because I can't just reveal how evil I can be but maybe you've seen through that already. You're more than just a baddie and I wish we can go steady. This is the new apocalypse I have to get ready for from within.

Stars At Sea

After fighting the Grand War both times, my body is weakened but my heart feels warm when I see a picture of you. I smile with a broken face when I hear your laugh in my vast memories. Before I left you told me to be strong, so I will be. You told me to be tough and I am going to be. I remember when you bopped your head against a table. I laughed and said how Nurse John will make it better with a kiss and if able to, maybe your lips, too. I can't bear to look at my broken face for I know my whole body is destroyed and ruined and only you can put me back together like glue. I've always loved you in that pink turtleneck with a pink bow on your hair but I withdrew so you wouldn't catch me staring. I remember your smile that lasts for a while but I look away because I feel guilty. I've taken the lives of so many and fired the guns at will because I was eager to win, to push through so I can get shipped to see you. The candle lights keep me company as the view of the night sky illuminates a constellation of you, your face with lights of the stars at sea. I can't even muster the energy to cry because it hurts just to breathe and I can't feel the leg missing, itching. You're so wholesome and I can't imagine life without you but get even more jealous when after I die you'll be with another kissing his lips away. I can't remember what year it is, but maybe this was the time when I made the pact again. I long for your touch, I long for your hugs, I want to see those eyes again and wish I can kiss you one more time, just once. I painfully turn my head and see the hourglass slipping its last piece of sand. Time's up and I can't even panic because I can't even stand. Goodbye until the next reincarnation.

Strange Siren

The girl with the eyebrow slit captivated me with her dark green eyes and red hair. She had a certain flair about her. Her dark lashes and nose rings is something I'm not usually in awe of but it isn't half bad at all and the liquor doesn't help at all. She's one of those sirens that hunts dirty souls in the Atlantic who will crawl to her will. She tried talking to me but I was too concentrated on what's ahead. She blew a kiss at me and tried to tempt me and tried to take me to bed. She seduced me and danced like a snake to me. When I finally gave in and kissed her gentle, thick innocent lips she screamed at me. She accused me of being fake and trying to use her because she knew she saw past my soul and even though I can be a bad guy it was too much for her to handle. A little black heart of gold would be too much of a scandal. I could see the panic in her eyes as I kissed her forehead and told her it's going to be okay. I held her in my arms and cradled her and heard her pray in soft whispers. Maybe she's just used to seeing the bad in people and sees the world in black and white, going blinder in the winter. She doesn't believe me, she doesn't think I'm real and I can feel her going mad. I gently lift her up and tell her I'm a nomad with no memory of the past but I'll be here for her if she wants me there. She feels that I'm being superficial and I can see her cold breath in the air. She's as pale as snow with eyes piercing more than a Scorpio's. Maybe I'm sympathetic but I'll go with the flow and row my boat towards the mainland. I'll use some of my power to heal her mentally and unbreak her heart.

Blood Red Moon

I see an angelic being floating above the full moon under the stars. I can feel his pain and I can see his scars. He has one on his eye, a vertical slit and I know he's fought harder than the god Mars. He's me. I can't tell if I'm dreaming but I know there's a sword on my chest. He's crying and I'm crying because we're both lying. Under the blood red moon that shines beyond the falling leaves the wind blows around. The clown that is me with a gaping wound on my heart. He extends his hand but I can't reach it for I'm too weak but I don't want to depart. He holds the answers I thought I needed, the answers to why but it doesn't make sense if I'm here and he's there. Am I seeing double or hallucinating? I struggle to get up, to see if I can get a closer look but he's illuminating facts that bright up the darkness in this forest. He reminds me of the soft kisses I once had, the gentle touches, the tight hugs and the sly looks I would love getting from the florist. I would give her little love notes and watch her read it while her cheeks flourish bright red. She would look at me and I could see how it had an effect on her with butterflies in her stomach. She would rush towards me and bombard me with kisses and everlasting hugs. When I look back at her I'm seeing the angelic monster wiping away my tears. He stares at the sword in my chest but doesn't remove it, he just smiles at me. He points at the sky and I feel the fear creeping in. The moon is bleeding, too. It's so red. He tells me to listen. "Listen to the voices in your head." Everything I knew or was it misread? He squeezes my hand but I have to keep my grip strong because it's comforting, I won't let him go. He places his hand on my head and I can hear what he means, a girl singing with an off tune melody of the crazies. Oh, God. Have I been misplaced or was this because of time traveling meddling? Confusion in my mind, I prepare for the upcoming nightmare.

Sleeping

It's a nice hot summer day, the cold sweat gone from the darkest winter of my life ends today. It's June 22 and it's my birthday. Rising up, rubbing my eyes, I look to the side and smile happily. I plant a good morning kiss on her cheek and start my day. What plans to make? What goals to take? All the gold, riches and wishes attained after fighting, stealing and destroying for so long, the darkest of sacrifices already made and perhaps it wasn't all fake. My love gets up to sing and dance with me, celebrating yet another victory of life as she surprises me with a cake. Her smooth, soft small hands touch the edges and curves of my body. She enjoys how lean I am and makes note of my clean outfit, ruffling up my wet hair and just smiles at me from cheek to cheek and is happy to be with somebody. After she gets ready, she drives us to a special place as she has me blindfolded without suffering as I feel the cool breeze from the car that embodies my giddiness. Finally arriving, she yanks off the blindfold to give me a kiss. It's a little get together masqueraded for two. She hired a hard working crew to build us a ship to go on a cruise and set sail whenever we want with the wealth we accrued. We sit back knocking off a couple of drinks and clinking merry wishes to each other and watch some birds fly through the air, soaring. She took my hand and kissed it, making me feel uneasy yet relaxed as my tensions and calamity settled from the scars of life. Pouring another drink for me I know life won't be boring. She picks me up to groove and move on the dance floor, making jokes along the way and laughing with her until my ribs hurt. She lets me do what I want with her, pleased with every touch and sentimental flirt. She eats up all the loving words I say to her and she's on high alert. She seduces me with her skirt and shakes it for me as I cheer her on, trying to keep up with her dance moves. She asserts her dominance over me and we gather a crowd up like we're a concert. She makes me blush and I can feel nervous but she calms me down, exciting me with butterflies in my belly and converts the energy to a soulful kind of love. Everything becomes fuzzy for a while but all that matters is that I'm with her. She plants a kiss on my forehead as if she was saying goodbye. When I open my eyes again, it's the dead of winter again and I look up, cursing at the sky. It was all a dream and I've been sleeping, hibernating and only having myself to rely.

Darkness in my Heart

I can hear the devils on my shoulders giving me the wrong answers. I can hear the whispers of my other bad half giving me temptations as they make their little advances. I'm in a room full of dancers. Cash everywhere, booze in my hand and I can't think straight and it's getting late. No final destination in mind, I walk out the door but I can't walk straight. Beggars wanting money from me but I push them aside. I've been unloved and mistreated just like you and I've tried. I don't care about your sentiments, you can leave them at home as I continue my stride. Hands deep in dirt, dirty deals and messy contracts applied. I'm the trendsetter at the center. No need to spread the terror because I'm the jester. Repairing my broken soul in exchange for the green as I clean up my mess with an old sweater. Always the aggressor, hiding behind pressure. I've been bossing it up since I was 23. Put down 8 times, I get up 9 times after the battle to clear the debris. I can't plead guilty because I'm free. I've got roadblocks in front of me because I can't tell what's real or what's fake, what really is authentic but I need to find the key. My heart is still black, there's a lot I still lack and the patience has run drier than the Nile river on a bad season. My soul has gone cold, I can feel it in my bones and I wonder where the love went, I need a reason to keep going. The worst treason is the one I've committed to, lying to myself and now I'm wheezing because I can't spit out the holy untruths that came out of my lips. It's all gone wrong but I can't shake it off, I'll have to dig myself out of this whole and vanquish life, choking it in my hands even if I have a little black heart.

Unsure

I remember when it was cold out, I covered you up in my winter jacket. It was heavy and just the right size to keep you warm like a little locket. You looked so cute bundled up in it and wearing it like a majestic cape and I wanted to hug you so badly, holding you tightly like a bracket. You're smile worthy and you're the right person with a description that can't be written up in a packet. Yes, I did meet you in the summer and the first words I tried to speak only came out in short stutters. It was embarrassing that your presence had such a powerful effect on me because I was a newcomer. I wanted to live up to your standards of perfection as I rambled through my brain beyond the clutter. I wanted to make it seem like I knew what I was doing but my legs became weak and melted like peanut butter. I would look at you and smile from afar, just thinking what you would be like and fast forwarding to now I do the same thing but at least I can be much closer to you. Whatever I say or do always makes you laugh, which is puzzling to me but I am happy to serve you like a loyal butler. Crushing on you hard for days on end, from weeks to months all because of little seeds planted on my mind. At first I thought little of it because I was busy being on my grind. Then our souls intertwined with vast similarities and unspoken energies that made me think twice because we were perfectly aligned. Confined with you is the best for me because spending most of my time being around you and with you feels right by design. I was lucky you were part of the outline because never in a million years would I ever thought something like this can happen but it is still undefined. Maybe all of this is behind a mastermind playing and moving little things that would eventually come to place as we make the perfect team, perfectly combined. I have gone crazy at times when I think and get locked up mentally but you remind me of me at times. The irony is that maybe you're the mirror reflecting me, a brighter and more wholesome version of what I can be. Unless you're not as kind as I am and can play off many versions of yourself, keeping the real you hidden and using the same tactics I use. I'm still unsure but I'll push the boundaries to see you.

Sensual Admiration

You're too sweet for words and it's absurd how I can't contain myself. You split me unevenly in two thirds, trying to guide me as a shepherd guides a herd. I can't tell exactly what I'm feeling and keeping it under wraps but then I let it go like a dam releasing water, overflowing because I can't contain myself and want to seduce you even if we are both reserved. I can stare at you all day and even if it's nasty your germs can be my germs because I'm down to be with you so I can nurse you back to health. I have gathered and amassed an impressive amount of wealth. That means nothing if I can't spend it with you for time I do not have. I want to grab you by the waist and dance around the room and remember the time when you asked me if I was waiting for you. I wanted to pick you off your feet and carry you to the moon to see the world with a different view. I want to show you how my soul burns for you, placing your hands on my head so you can see the images and read my mind with your psychic gifts. Your gifted perceptions and intuition can pick up on this so I can treasure you and lift you up and take my time being swift. You're a gem and deserve to be cultivated and take time as you make me slow down and drift along the sidelines. I know you can appreciate my body, my sculpted curves and I will let you touch me if it's alright with you. Those brown pairs of eyes can make me die with just one sight of them. Everyday I make myself better to be worthy of you. Tell me, remove my doubts and let me speculate, are your actions and subtle phrases pertain to what I hope it is or am I just your favorite? Can I keep hoping for a brighter tomorrow helplessly as I smile like an idiot when I remember what we did or am I crazy to savor it? They call me beautiful inside and out and can charm my way into you because I'm just like you in so many ways that seem insignificant at first but maybe it's meant to be. You always laugh at the things I say, the little chuckles lift my spirits up just a bit with your impressive smile that leaves me dumbfounded. They say you sometimes nod and smile when they talk about me and don't bother to deny it when they instigate a little rumor. I admire your sense of humor because it's sadistic and twisted as mine, choking me harder than a tumor. Your quiet demeanor is broken when I open my mouth and you entertain me at times, with little trinkets of words spilled. You satisfy me just by touching and holding me, encouraging words and even when you are defeated it gives me room to comfort you back in return. I love this sweet and slow burn. I don't mind it at all when you're so close to me we bump legs and shoulders without concern. You always extend the vowels of my name and worry about me at times to the point where I get confused if it's curiosity or genuine sentiment. You come through and join the conversations and jokes which can mean you're playing it off just to be near me or maybe I'm overthinking again. I don't know where all this is coming from. I'm such a stuttering clown when it comes to you and other times I can act arrogantly but you don't seem to mind and I can't think of a reason why. You chime in once in a while and are always smiling around me when I'm close by. Apparently I'm more animated as you giggle and laugh at my stories. You are way more than what meets the eye. You're a puzzle I can't solve, keeping me guessing all the time. I get sad when we have to say goodbye but I'm excited when I look at my watch knowing we will see each other again that quantifies the intensity.

Victory

It doesn't seem like much now, but the sense of slow winning has crept upon me unbeknownst to all of us. It didn't take a magic school bus, it didn't take money, it didn't even take an ounce of regret but pure luck and there's plenty to discuss. I never have believed it yet I have felt and known this whole time. I was still worried about the predetermined obstacle I scoffed at because I am well beyond my prime. They call me Superman in the daytime and Batman when it's grim as if it was a crime. Stepping to the test, stepping up to the plate to make things fall in place, ripe and rhyme so my soul can chime. This bittersweet victory tastes better than champagne because it came unexpectedly and with a new plan in motion, I can step forward like a knight, bow down to my new queen, my new empress, the enchantress, the goddess that will help me ascend beyond the possibilities of being superior. There never was an ulterior motive because on the exterior I was genuine as I was on the interior. We never saw it coming, ignoring the signs and messages from the notes above that fell down to our earth that broke the barrier. Maybe I am delusional and crazy but this victory makes me think otherwise. Despite my size, I still control the space and attention from the people when I walk in the room. The lies they spread, the compromise I had to make, to realize the surprise when I heard the news and to not act on it will be unwise. We both will immortalize whatever this is, beyond the depths of anyone's understanding and make it clandestine but universally understood by all. I will do nothing to jeopardize this, trust me because all the moves have been placed in such a fashion. Check mate. Never have I ever been so motivated from being hopeless to now imagine a future I thought I would have to work much harder for. Maybe this is what sets me apart from the malicious version of what I can be, opening a new door for endless shores. The victory from the supposed boy next door.

I Thought I Knew

When you told me you asked about me and wondered where I was at, I had no idea what was in store for me and I wished I gave you a tight, brief hug and continued the chat. I didn't realize it at the time and I should have picked up on it but I lacked intuition and I wish I had that. You're like no other but maybe I say that about everyone but I think about you all the time even in the threat of a gun. Run around my mind, the endless thoughts of you in endless curiosity as I look at the sun momentarily and when I look at you, I am stunned. I stuttered words that couldn't come out right and now I make you laugh effortlessly and it fuels my appetite. There's a lot you do to me that ignites a light in me I thought I've sealed away and I the curves, inches of your body, shapely chinky eyes, voluptuous lips and a gorgeous smile I can recite. I imagine countless ways of being with you but when reality hits, I scurry away to not make a scene because it's way worse than playing with fire but perhaps you can enjoy the spotlight. I can hear your voice and hum in my mind. I love to hear in the real world and it's like a little beacon light. They say Scorpios have trust issues and for whatever godforsaken reason you trust me, it brings a joyful smile that makes me warmer than the increasing Fahrenheit. I lay down with my head in the clouds and replay the same words, expressions and way too similar qualities we share, blending in the crowd so perfectly. I guess you're the one I've been praying for, manifesting in a totally different being I never thought possible. You have me begging for you at times and you don't even know it but I'm sure your advanced intuition can detect it and it's not an omission. If I were to be near death's door with a terminal illness, the sight of you will put me in remission. I can feel your soul touching mine and I look away at times, hoping you'll stare back at me into submission. I'll keep my sweet gaze at you as you smile back at me, pretending nothing is going on with your serious manner that clouds what you might feel inside. I can hear your giggles as we wrap arms, clinched as we walk around synchronized. I love it when you ask me for favors because I know I won't disappoint you and if I make a little mistake, you laugh at it and let it slide. You're always thanking me for my help and no matter what I say or do, you laugh as I am puzzled but it makes me happy anyway because I want to be alongside you for this entire ride. You laughed each time when I told you I would betray others just to stay with you and you approved, which quantified the quality of the contract I had with you. You repeat some words I say with hidden emphasis that make me giddy secretly. I thought I knew but maybe this long and slow process will make you gravitate towards me and this will be a new world wonder, even stranger than déjà vu.

Wedge Wolf

I am to be deployed tomorrow but I'm not entirely in sorrow. The bottle of wine helps ease the pain, a gift of the fallen pharaoh. We have been thorough in this war and I've been the antihero for this show. Countless times I have seen many fall as I am the only one who can't die. An endless life forever, I'll always need to resupply. I stare outside the window, eons ahead of time, the future with neon lights that glimmer the city with no ally. I don't know what it is you want from me. You open the lines of communication just to ignore me. Are you giving me orders to test my patience? Do you truly want to be my friend or do you just want to use me? That's my speciality. I keep my head down and they all like me because I'm obedient. Maybe I'm being too linenat. Trespasses committed against me but when I give them a taste of their own medicine they're going to be in shock. They'll ask me why I betrayed the state. I've been doing what you've done, so how is it any different? Two can play at that game, considering all that has been done to me again and again. For all my experience and years in combat, I am still too naive and this is far too rigorous. I haven't learned from past mistakes but I keep on advancing in rank, whispering. I am the Wedge Wolf where the enemy fears behind cracks of armies and doesn't dare to say my name, suffering. I have been betrayed and scarred by those close to me but it doesn't matter because I'll bring vengeance, delivering. To do what I'm told, to complete my mission, to seduce, charm and destroy to bring home the intel in ignorance. What am I really fighting for? Is it for the greater good, the cause or myself? The undying loyalty I can't find in other soldiers hungry for fame and fortune. They've shot and stabbed me in the back only for me to get up and shoot them back, eyes wide open staring into mine. I've seen the soul leave their bodies. Such a tragedy. I'm trapped in this conscience. I'm trapped in this body, in this mind and the only thing I can do is move onward. When they need me they'll come for me and I, stupidly, will come to their aid in their beck and call. That's only when they show up and not bother to check up on their beloved soldier. I'll come like a hungry dog waiting to be commanded and do their bidding. They love me just for that and I'm not sure how long I'll be up for it. Arms wide open and happy to help them only to be ripped apart where I have to pick up the pieces. If it was too much for you, why didn't you say so? If you miss me why don't you say so and act on it? If you told me you cared about me why doesn't it feel like it? If we haven't talked in so long, why don't we talk,not ignoring me instead of briefing me for a mission where I am sent behind enemy lines to wipe them all out? If you didn't want to ruin what we have, why did you let us step out of line and do it over again and again? Why haven't you stopped me? Stepping into virtual reality to ease my mind and meditate, I have to seek the calmness in this calamity. Questions I don't have the leisure of getting as I set sail aboard the ship, shooting away angel fire at the enemy. You'll see. Maybe I'm just too good for you and I'll set my own path, a revolution where I will become the bourgeoisie. I won't be broken, I won't be torn down and I won't throw it all away for anyone ever again. Maybe not yet, maybe not now, eventually when I get older and when I'm tired of being resurrected over and over to fight an old man's war is when I'll take action. Maybe tomorrow. Maybe now. Maybe next year I'll disappear and you'll never see me again until you wake up from a dream and stare down my eyes through the barrel of my firearm. My true identity will be forgotten and only be remembered as the Wedge Wolf. Forget my kindness, forget my brightness, forget my talents, forget my wishes. I'll be waiting in silence until I wreak havoc tomorrow. I'll erase every memory from you about me and it'll be glorious. It was an honor to serve you but a greater honor to serve myself.

Angel Fire

Set sail to the dangers that lie ahead, it happened too fast and the soldiers that were with me are now dead. On the way I thought to myself, what happens when people leave? They can leave an empty space in you for a long time to grieve or help you build a garden that'll blossom all that you can achieve. An insane battle between two opposing factions, bullets firing everywhere and the sand turned maroon from the dried up blood that will deceive you. For what seemed like forever, taking down the adversaries for a long time I saw her. A brave woman fighting on her own, holding her own with her sword, shield and rifle. Crazy combinations only taught me when I was a boy but she did it so amazingly that it was perfectly in tune to whatever song she had in her head, a seamless choreography that ripped the numbers down. Her strong shoulders and lean body flowing perfectly with muscles that were appealing, beautiful to look at and I can feel the touch and see how strong she is. She looked back at me, awaiting for my command as I closed in on her, back to back with opponents all around. I had given her a brief instruction and a pattern that was practiced and rehearsed before and I saw her frown go upside down. She thought exactly like me, made the same expressions and said the same things as I as time slowed down. We were one and the same, two soldiers fighting in synchronicity together as this battlefield became our playground. There was no other perfect team than the present moment as we adjusted slight patterns of a strange yet similar variety as the soldiers became a forgotten noun. She protects, she attacks, but most importantly she never lacks. Her galant enthusiasm and confidence makes her do her job so well that she draws back a mortal wounding lunge that makes them step back. Throwing a flash bang, we ran for higher ground to pick off the foes as we had the same idea without saying a word to each other and I know she can be a part of my pack. She does her little grown woman laugh as victory is imminently ours as I crack a little joke, hearing her sweet chuckle gives me a chance to feel just right. We have a knack for this. Reading each other's minds and knowing what to do, we launched explosives that rained hell on them that burned them and destroyed them just right to smite. We high fived each other for a successful campaign, holding the gaze in each other's eyes and interlocking hands for a brief moment that made us feel as if each of us were a knight. The mother of all ships blocked the sky and made it turn night. Their launch pods slammed into the ground with combatants armed to the teeth to murder the two mercenaries but our crazy selves were in such delight. I saw her cute mouth form symmetrical dimples and knew the pain we would give them will hurt more than a frostbite. The outcome will come to our hands easily and outright.

Subtle

We laugh and stand so close, arms touching and I'm tempted to hold your hand as you discuss the plans for the day. You stand and instruct me what to do and I pay so much attention that I make sure not to stray. I look at the information on display but I also study your hand, the traces of your sweet fingers and I just want to grab them and kiss each bone of your finger to the palms of your hands but I'm worried of what you might say. I want to lay my head on your shoulder and although some may not agree you might be the one for me. They want us to be a thing and I can't disagree. Sitting down today when you were instructing, I studied every part of your body. I loved the shapes of your shoulders as you confidently stood tall to the way your little forearms looked so adorable that way. I loved seeing the veins that pumped around them, strong and healthy. The dress you had on silhouettes your body shape perfectly. I loved the way your hair looked and I just wanted to kiss you, waiting for everyone to leave and press my lips on your neck and cheeks as you play and pull my hair. Sometimes I say the wrong thing and you make a scowl looking face but then I remember you can also say some dark things and laugh every time I speak without a care. You don't mind me at all and I love it but we have to keep pretending because this is something we can't spare. We make the perfect pair. I can help you organize the thoughts and things in your life and even then you say it'll still be discombobulated but I beg to differ, yes I dare. Sitting so close to you I've traced your mouth and wrinkles from your face with my fingers and I can feel your warm skin with my gentle touch with you on that chair. With my little jokes around and you sarcastically reply by saying, "very funny" as we move around with our cherished footwear. I can't get enough of you and I long to spend my golden hours with you and I feel a special type of feeling when you ask me if I'm fine or if I'm hungry, it shows you care. It can be the basic kind of human decency but it's too valuable for me because my welfare is as important as yours. I cheer you on as you celebrate your small victory but I wish I encouraged you more because you're always smart to me, not just sometimes because even you have taught me many things. The way you act around me is so subtle and I wonder at times yet others catch on but then I get frustrated and confused but you make me sing. You told my superior that you are beyond glad and grateful to have me around because you wouldn't know how you would be able to do this alone and I think how that would be possible or if it's really true. She tells me that whatever I do or don't do seems to be magical because it controls the miniature zoo. My energy matches with just about any of them and you know damn well it matches with yours, too. I hope you're not just being too friendly and maybe have some sort of crush on me, too, because you're just my favorite and meet me for a rendezvous. Sometimes your vengeful acts remind me of something I would do, especially when Sparta kicked someone as I threw my head back and laughed hard enough that my ribs would be in pain at this view. Water sign gang unite, that's us and the more I think about this review, I feel like it can be something true. I've just got to play my cards right and continue the build up but hope I'm not crazy. I just want...you.

Wonders

A meeting with the board, you didn't have much to say and for them to look down on you I couldn't afford. I jumped in the nick of time to save you just a tiny bit discreet enough to not lord over you. My head is always in the clouds and I get so lazy, drowsy when I think of you and walking towards you will be my reward. You make me laugh when you speak in a silly British accent on purpose that throws me off and you like the little magicians that makes me think twice as I search up tickets using the keyboard. You seemed stressed out with things I want to help with not because I'm bored. There was a story a little one wrote as a gift to me where I am the jester and you are the princess and we cross paths towards one another. In her story she says we are quite different yet the chemistry is unspoken but seen by all but we have to remain undercover. The little scribe told me that we always matched in such a gracious manner. When you're with others it isn't the same because when I come back it's like we never left each other and fit perfectly like pieces to a puzzle. You act so cool and collected at times and I can't figure you out, just hoping that I can dream forever as the little one manifests things with her magical ink. I blink back the daydream and see you pouting at me because there is so much to do in so little time. I'd love to ask you out for a drink, add sour like to your coke and rum. I'd love to have you on my arm as we explore the city and wander into museums of all sorts and take in the history and arts of civilization and talk about the place you're from. I'm dying to send you little cute messages that will make you laugh, melt your heart and be reassured that I've got your back in the dark times of this massive plague. I'm strategizing a way to get closer to you without coming off too strong or inappropriate but the options are just so vague. I'm using many genies to find a way to give me a genuine and brilliant idea to arrive at a suitable solution. You're a daydream wrapped in a human body with a soul like ice cream wrapped and protected around a black shield to fend off the users and liars.

Light Skinned Temptation

Can't keep my emotions under control. I've been bad at handling and tried to put it like a sprawl. I'm doing everything I can not to sell my soul. When I look at you I glance away because I'm a shy boy. Other times I'm cocky and make my facade so real even you get infected with joy. I don't want to hurt you but you squeeze me so tightly even just for a second and that I enjoy. I have enough strength to break you in half so I have to be gentle and do my best not to destroy. I want to keep you in a loving death grip as you keep me in but I know you're not a toy. I want to make a pinky promise to you but to honor it entirely will not be my greatest struggle. I want to have you to snuggle. You fall asleep early because you're so overworked and mumble in your sleep. I want to keep you in my arms so I can kiss your forehead but I'm troubled. You're the light skinned temptation but I want to keep my employment. I don't wish to endanger you or risk what you love doing the most but what if we both are humble? I can't wait for the manifestations to come true because the wishes have been coming to reality lately. The little ones spoke it into existence and it's okay if they jinxed it because I appreciate it greatly. I am without words because I'm not sure exactly how to say it because I do know what to say. All I can do now is keep planting the seeds as I push the literal obstacles out the way because they root for me, have faith in me. I want to tell it to you straight: I want you eternally. It's okay if you don't feel the same way. I just still remain hopeful even then because I'm crazy. I laugh when you say I do just about everything and how I stand on the ceiling to help educate those that might eradicate. I'm subtle but even you must know you're just my favorite in the whole wide world even if I'm not in the right mental state. I sit back and observe for a while but I lack to make eye contact. My eyes just wander off as if they have a mind of its own but I'm glad I always have you howling hysterically and I love to keep track. You always have this stupid grin or wide smile when you see me, giving a casual hi when I'm walking back, minding my business with thoughts about you no matter how hard I distract myself. Don't you know you're worth more than an artifact? You poke fun at yourself from time to time but I'm busy chuckling that I can't even defend you from yourself because even at a short distance you bring a powerful impact. It doesn't matter how hard I meditate, how much weight I push to tire myself out, spending time with friends I never thought I'd make, you're always on my mind and your name spews out my mouth. No matter what I do I can't subtract you from me in any way. I'm just waiting to see how you react. I act so oddly, childishly yet manly at other times all at once because I haven't fully accepted it yet. The light skinned temptation I'm trying to resist but fail amicably because you are just like me.

90s Baby

Hands all over, you're like my four leaf clover. You brighten up my day when I walk in the room, just endless thoughts of you and you've come to take over. With you I feel like I don't have to compete, I don't have to worry with glances over my shoulder and you make me feel good inside. You're a 90s child like me and you always let me slide. I don't know what's true and I know it doesn't have to be true because my mind is a lie and this is a nice fantasy. It's like Zack Morris and Lisa Turtle from Saved by the Bell with a deep agony. We have so much in common, so much chemistry but it's a dangerous game but we can rule the galaxy. Everybody is dying to see us together just for a moment like a love story you see on TV. I've been called fearless because I don't care about the consequences and nearly everybody knows yet I am very lucky. We are nearly the same, maybe exactly the same in all the vanity. You and I...where did you come from, exactly? I've always wondered what a female counterpart of me would be like and here you are, what a manifestation of reality. You make me smile because I want you to stop it, thinking like me, talking like me, reacting like me. You're a running riot with those smoky chinky eyes that mean everything when you look at me and even use the same profanity. Are you crazy or am I? Why are we like this? The zodiacs can't match perfectly as for a reason that your psychology is nearly identical to mine. I can wrap my tired arms around your waist while you squeeze my back powerfully. When you're with me you are much more lively. Is this a fact? Are we to keep this pact? You agreed that I sacrifice everything and everyone for you, for a little notebook that just may create a future legacy. We both dress similarly in the outlooks of 90s minimalists. Things you say and do remind other people of me, isn't that sweet? You remind them of me...words that cannot be placed yet it's a great treat. I'm looking at a mirror but the reflection is you, little one, are you the one I'm supposed to meet? You grab my hands through the mirror and pull me in gently and dance with me like a crazy person in your suite. You laugh and act just like me, a fool trapped in a young person's mindset and attitude with hopeful pessimism unbalanced with insane optimism. I look at you and look at you and wonder again where it is you came from and when will your lips touch mine. I'm sweet on you like a kid catching a case of a sweet tooth with their favorite candy. Are you going to be my Hershey bar no matter how hard I push these feelings away? Am I going to be trapped inside you like an Oreo cookie? My head is spinning as I take control of the wheel but I must ask this: if I take a bite and a lick from you, will it be like having a kit kat bar? Maybe when you kiss my cheek, you can feel the delicate, soft skin as you own me momentarily before you regain composure. Put this to the test, I'll be like Nike… believe in something even if it means sacrificing everything, just do it. Toss a coin, flip the coin, I'll take my chances 50/50 to see what happens.

Just like Me

I wait outside leaning against the wall all cool. I think a lot about lately and I become so zombified I begin to drool. You're always coming in a rush because you can be forgetful due to many things racing on your mind like a depthless pool. I keep saying how alike we are because I never knew narcissism would manifest as a being like you, mirroring me, a female me, a counterpart in every way like a caveman discovering for the first time a useful, sharp tool. I didn't have to cut my own wings as they took time to grow again, following the golden rule. Every so often you say I'm the best and I have a stupid looking grin like a child being praised. Your little trophy that collects tears that are still warm scares and inditimates them but I find so much humor in that and I'm just so amazed. You torture them mentally, psychologically while I torture them physically, painfully. They saw we make sense and how we are the perfect duo. Crazy, right? You seemingly have many stressful bad days but I'm here to make them better, I want to be that one thing in your darkness that shines bright. I can wrap my strong arms around your small waist, catching you by surprise with panicking thoughts but you know it feels right. The heat we contract can turn into passion that burns like electric jolts with your touch that shocks every cell in my body with such delight. I think we play this game of being distant to see who caves in first just to be sure who will make the first move, who will make the moment a key highlight. Even I have called you crazy jokingly because you're like me in so many ways I can't fathom. With every touch, every hug, every longing look I steal away, planting seeds in your mind for a potential paradise. I make you laugh so much and let me get away with everything where others laugh at the ridiculous outcomes of it, where they feel I demoralize them. I try to help them but it's as if I ruin them on purpose, laughing wholeheartedly where I am a conspiracy to them. The oracle told me we will blossom in late March or late Spring, let's see if it's true. I don't let you finish your sentence all the way because I am way ahead of you, darling, my thoughts are your thoughts, twins in a way and let's see what this can become. Our strange and unspoken relationship is the perfect spice of life, adding flavor to the bystanders to where they root for me without concern of yours, yet you don't deny it, do you? Why? I can't know for sure. I'm sure you know but yet do you really? There's never a right time for this because it was unexpected yet came about ideally. I don't know what to do but to follow my heart, my instincts even if I feel silly.

Without Remorse

It's like I can't even express myself anymore without you getting angry at me. You judge others for not letting you be. You do the same to me. You risk pushing others away for reasons I don't understand, for pulling away so far from reach and it's tiring, to say the least. I've opened my eyes. It's night time and I'm here, it's raining. The cold liquid touches my face, icy sparkles of water across my skin. I see the ghost but he isn't talking to me. The ghost that is me. The ghost that is scared of me. It knows all of my sins, he wants to eat my soul. A look at his diamond eyes. Such anger! How demented! The spirit asks me, "are you like those arrogant people?" I laugh at his face and I tell him this, "those people you speak ill of are my family. Of course I'm arrogant. I'm the aristocrat lost in time. I am the perfect son. I am the favored one. I am a bit older than Herod, don't you know? I'm the price." The night sky blackens and it rains harder, becomes colder. I can hear people crying, screaming. I see the shadows of my past. The ghost is part of me. The one with the sparkling gem eyes is a reminder of the humanity I lost. He implored me to return to the way I was. I refuse. He begs me for food because he wants to eat me. He reminds me of simpler times, happier times, reminding me of the multiple times I have fallen in love. I don't want it back because my life is eternal, I am an immortal. I trick the ghost, offering up my life to him with arms wide open. He's glad that I have given up and before he can kill me, I use my final strength to rip out his eyes and swallow the spirit whole.

Where Were They?

One minute I'm talking to you, next thing I know there's a war going on. I can feel the fear and frustration. I see death, I see fire, I see captivity, all those around me gunned down for no good reason. Why? I can hear the angels weeping, crying, for they can not intervene for the times have locked them out of this misery. The dead rise from the virus of toxic humanity. I can hear their chants. Release the gods to slay the demon. Where were the destroyers when we needed them? The agony and sorrow mixed with my insane amount of rage releases. The tears I have to shed yet again for the losses. I am the strongest, my little heart's on fire for its blazing and this...this is war. The invaders that are too greedy to even comprehend what is going on. They tore down my home, they tore down the flags, they tore down my friends, my loved ones. Flying head first into battle with a seemingly indestructible body, I get rid of the soldiers. Their weapons of mass destruction have no effect on me. A weary body that gets stronger through pain. I release a beam towards their planes and tanks. My rage knows no bounds as I shoot flames from my mouth to take down the riflemen. A loud boom cracks from a distance but I'm too fast, the sniper missed and it strokes against his ego. Next thing I know, I land a wild haymaker to his skull and down he goes. I can hear the communications through their radio satellite as I launch up there at full speed, making the earth shake, crumbling the platform I was on and making headway through it in outer space. I catch the satellite and bring it with me to throw it at the enemy. I can see the military intervening to come to my aid because they were no match. More casualties I cannot endure. I can feel the knot in my throat as I wasn't fast enough to save them. I crash down creating a seismic wave that makes them lose balance. Slamming down their heads into the ground, I can feel it crush in my palms like squashing fruit. They scream in fear as I yell like a maniac on the street, running wildly I tackle another one as they frantically throw grenades at me with no effect. I walk towards them as they call me a monster repeatedly, bullets deflecting off me. I break their guns as if it were a broomstick and I can hear them call for retreat but I will take no prisoners. They will pay for what they have done. I will avenge them.

Those Feelings

I've been laying in bed just reminiscing the day you held me tightly, arms wrapped tightly to a strong squeezing point around my back. I fade to black. We lay our heads on each other's shoulders as I try to be gentle and measure my strength, my arms neatly wrapped protectively around your waist and I have a knack for making people easily trust me. I can imagine you one day surprising me, wrapping your arms around my waist, kissing my neck and cheeks whispering sweet words to my ears. You're warm, I can feel your heartbeat pulse steadily yet rapidly, trying to hide it, holding back the emotions you wanted to give away for years. You got so excited when I gave you the memorable gift, a meaningful that didn't have to be cheap earrings or an expensive necklace, doing a little dance with a grin that defeated me, putting an end to my miseries. I can't forget it and I refuse to delete the memory, like a happy little girl who got a pony for her birthday. You hugged me again and I felt the strength and gratitude, maybe this is something that happens once in a lifetime or just rarely. The next day you had on the special shirt that mirrored the gift, doing your hair to which was subtle but I might just have caught on, sincerely. Maybe one day this will be true, I want to just hold you and kiss you softly. I want you to call me your babe and be yours and stare at each other longingly. I probably had this come to me in a dream but I didn't remember it, seeing it before my eyes without remembering but I was glad you couldn't handle your feelings calmly. They say the world is ending and how I should just straight up tell you how I feel but despite everything, I remain optimistically hopeful. You'll come to me at the right time as I crossed destinies with yours at the right time. I keep picturing future scenarios with us together, laughing and exploring new things and I can't shake them off just yet and I don't even have to rhyme. Your chuckles make my day, seeing you smile at me cheers me up, but I wish I smiled back because I'm always dumbfounded and do a little grin. I wonder if my stoic and serious demeanor puts you off as if I were sin. You know I act silly naturally. I'm always on with the jokes even if I'm dying inside, a disease that cannot be cured physically. It's cured the day we both say, "I love you." Right now I'll keep taking the medicine, spitting off the blood in secret and treating the symptoms as all the doctors in the world couldn't help me. It's all done mentally. I can hold out as long as it takes because I've trained myself to live under these harsh conditions, fundamentally. If you're not the one, it's okay. It's just nice for now, knowing that I can keep on dreaming momentarily. It's what keeps me going day by day when money means nothing if I don't have the time to spend it with you. The only time I can do that is when I make money, so it's worth everything so far. All this happening accidentally, thinking constantly how this was possible. I guess what they say is true, the more time you spend with those around you that feelings can be caught at the end of a fishing rod that reeled in a princess in a sea of mermaids and I may have just gotten lucky.

Love in Sickness

They say I should reach out to you because we don't know when we'll see each other again. Quarantined and miles apart, I wish I can escape this den. The full moon is now and I transformed into a beast, roaming emotionally all around going insane. It's only been a couple of days but I miss you already with this longing pain. I feel as if we finally picked up on the flow and momentum. You asked me if I was staying, maybe you were hiding

your eagerness and I winced, only to say I would be gone for a short while.
I love it when you're around me, clinging unto me just for a second where
I can feel your warmth. They say it will be a few weeks until we return and
I thrash around like a child because that is too long for me, I can't go for so
long without seeing you smile and laugh in person but we can't be
misinformed. I wonder what it is you'll think and feel when I said I'll be
here for you should you ever need anything even if I have to walk through
this storm for you. I'll bring you a large care package, sacrificing
everything in my path just to make sure you're alright. I can't help but be
less subtle than you but I wonder if you don't mind it because I love the
smile of yours that burns bright. I don't know why you haven't called me
out on it or get me in trouble when I get distracted, maybe I have you
smitten as well, maybe just right. It'll be the longest 35 days ever but
maybe it'll be worth it because we don't know what the world holds, a
dangerous place and to solve its issues, I just wish it would go by quickly
each night to think of you first when there's sunlight. I wish to be there
with you, snuggling with you at all hours in this entrapment and when you
wake up in the morning, I'll be there still. All I have for now are these little
things I call hope and patience up until the day I see you again I'll squeeze
you powerfully as you do me, lift you up, spin you around and steal a kiss,
finally.

American Girl

The city that never sleeps is the place we live in. I want to sleep next to
you, crawl in your bed and bring you thousands of smooches. Classic,
erratic, young and fearless would be me while you're more careful,
precautious, prudent but even you can be childish like me. Show me what's
around your block and we can go for a nice walk and have deep talk. You
can ruffle up your hands in my hair, feel how soft it is as I look nervously
at you, studying your cheek bones, the wrinkles of your grin, being close
enough to kiss your neck but make it a tease. You study my thick body
shape under my clothes and my overrated Ultra Boosts. I make little jokes
about your 1's and you're always chuckling at what I have to say, a victim
of the 90s. I'm paler than a Caucasian, an accent of a Hispanic with a
tongue that matches no other and able to translate four other languages.
You're a delicious light skin with curly hair I want to touch, slender body

shape but strong enough to beat me up if you had to, I'll like it when you vanquish me. I love your distinct accent when you talk, I pretend not to swoon when I look at you and can imitate it when you're not around. You don't really say much but you don't have to because we seem to always be on the same page. I can't believe I wrote about you so many times now but I'm glad because you're more than a muse to me I want to engage. I want to pick you up, play a sweet tune and dance with you on stage. You're the crush I never knew I wanted and it doesn't matter if we aren't the same age. A dangerous game of chess and chicken, flying too close to the sun might cause damage. I secretly stare at you when you walk with a sexy strut and we always bump into each other, giggling and saying hi as if nothing happened like we are teenagers. I want you to grab me by the shoulders, wrap your hand on my bicep to have you running around inside, shy enough to do so but I want you to crave me. I want to wrap my arm around your shoulder even if it feels heavy on you. I want you to feel protected by my brute strength, silver tongue mannerisms and intelligent ways, enthralled by my presence and infatuated with me as I am with you. I love how intimidating you can make me feel, always a mystery and keeping my mouth shut before I say something stupid because you seem way too real for me, a daydream walking towards me with your piercing eyes that just do it for me. I can appear to be suave and nonchalant despite my Peter Parker tendencies while you're like this perfect mixture of Catwoman and Wonderwoman, confident yet humble where you don't mind making fun of yourself. There's a lot on your pretty mind and disorganized to the point where even if I helped it wouldn't do much. Your short temper, stress and patience are tested on the daily but as I keep repeating, that's where I come in to make your day better. I can hold you by the waist and fly away to a fortress of solitude, enjoying dinner paired with candle lights, holding hands and having a good time. You can even challenge me to an arm wrestling match just to test your strength, use two hands as we laugh hysterically. I want to be your American boy and I want your beautiful and exotic self for me.

Twist the Knife

A century old, a vampire I am. Still young and new to do this but I've lived for so long without a true love so I had to make it up by taking these milligrams. I drink blood just to live but do I live like a lamb? I'm not exactly meek but the misfortunates have been much more than my blessings, devoting my life and love for people who just don't give a damn. I drew an ideal diagram. None of them cared because I'm not part of their program. Waiting for people who can't sacrifice just a bit for me, so I lure them in to drink their life away. I remove their pain to make it easy for them as I increase my own life force as I avoid the sun some days. I walk alone in the night, feeling satisfied with my late night dinner but my body is still cold. I want to lay in bed with someone to cuddle, not another dead body. I fall in the same trap, same mistake when I act human. Snowflakes that melt into tears drop down my cheeks as my demonic, icy blue eyes show the disillusion, deep dejection and gloom easily. Even my smiles can not hide the sadness I feel deep inside, so I dance around the fire and act as if nothing affects me. I have a drink with the devil as we share back for the poor souls we have tricked, the souls we sold in exchange for empty promises. I can't tell if the green or hazel eyes look back at me longingly and wish if they truly want to marry me or if they will leave me at the altar or if they accuse me of being the scum who was an assaulter. It doesn't matter how much whiskey and wine I drink. It doesn't make me feel any better, it doesn't numb the pain, it doesn't make the void in my soul become full as it did some time ago. Another neck drained of blood, two little holes that don't resemble an animal attack of any kind. I want you to feel my pain, I want you to feel my sadness, I want you to cry with me because my own tears have dried out. When you explain to someone how much you love them and how much they hurt you and how it can be better just for them to do it to you, how does it feel? For them to tell you how much in pain they are, how many times they have been betrayed, how many times they have been hurt and lied to but they do it to other people? Tell me, what remedy is there? Revenge, perhaps. I play with their minds and tell them to come to me, with tears in my eyes I do the world a favor by removing and sucking the blood of yet another flaky, superficial, selfish, prejudice person who made me second guess every action and word because I could have sworn they cared about me or at least respected me but you played me more than you played yourself. The emotions there that you've shown me only to pull back, and when it hurts me more to take a bite out of your neck, taking your soul, I can't hold back the memories we created, having the best moments I wish I can have again. As your body falls lifelessly with a loud thud, I look at my reflection and think back how I've done the same long ago. This is my karma but I can't let it go. I can't be a victim if I'm the one doing the actual hurting. I didn't care. I still care. Maybe my love is toxic, kills anything it touches and destroys completely like how a drought ruins a beautiful flower. Maybe it's better that you avoid me, doing better if we never cross paths or never have met me. It doesn't matter now because I have no power in changing the past. Being unloved for so long is as damaging as a person with a mental illness, a person dying of cancer, worse than a chronic smoker and as bad as an emotional rollercoaster of a day drinker. There is nothing to do but to muster the strength to go forward. The skeletons in my closet have taken extra space, requiring another closet to lock these things away. The chains become weaker. Look at me, you see a young boy. Look into my soul you see an old black soul trying to fit in and make sense in all this. I am always hungry and no amount of blood will fill my sustenance, nothing to quench my thirst and no hope to feel human again. Yes, being at my most vulnerable and open to risk it all but I'm too old to do it. Even if you give me true death by meeting the sun at its prime, I still cannot die because I will just rise from the ashes at night. What resolution will there be? Nobody knows.

Beat Faster

The first time I saw you, I felt stupid because I stuttered. No words would come out as I tried to make sense but my mind just cluttered. I extended my hands out with my heart beating so fast I couldn't hear properly what your name was, I was worried I wasn't myself or if I squeezed your hand way too tightly. I couldn't make sense of this and I tried to stick to the program but I tried to act politely. I looked all innocent and tried to keep my dirty thoughts inside because those curves matched your body and demeanor nicely. I saw those mysterious eyes that looked way past into my soul and into my future and I wondered if you were a descendant of Aphrodite. The lips that are full and picturesque, soft and tender, delicate with a scowl that I loved to look at when you spoke sweetly. I can't remember what those summer days were but there is a pattern of the magic in the hotter days that lifts me heavily. I wished I stayed longer to help you and manage your headaches as I would leave early and say not to let this job stress you out which was unlikely. I wish I had photographic memory. I would tune in and laugh, smile, and feel butterflies exponentially. I would remember every emotion, nervousness, anxiety, every word spoken and every chuckle from the day we met to every thought I had of you. It felt as if those two weeks and a half was everything for you to request my help in the future, unbeknownst to me of the small impact I had. Maybe we clicked but didn't realize it, maybe it was the deep chemistry I never saw coming, funny because that's what she said, and it was an unspoken truth and now I'm just really glad. Maybe it's selfish but no matter how much I dig past the paradigm of my memories, I can't recall much but the important little details that transformed you into something much more than a comrade. Maybe tonight I can dream of the time from the early days we worked with each other to solve the equations that would help people from destroying themselves and to pass the rite of passage. Now I just look forward eagerly to spending time with you, just to hear you ask me if I'm staying over or not and I pretend we're riding down a carriage in the park with white horses. You crept in my mind a few times but I didn't think much of it because I had to deal with the morbid corpses I had within me but you're just enormous. You bring such a presence and you've become a special being that penetrated my heart and it's your rareness. I stare at the ceiling just remembering you, how you reacted and what you said so I can feel my spirit clap and cheer. It's almost 11:11 and I know damn well I'm wishing for you yet again, another night, four minutes away. I wrote wishes down in a ripped piece of paper and hid it underneath my pillow. You told me to tell you if they come true which I will do. It's a secret I shared to you, and trust me, when it does happen you will be the first to know. Two minutes to the count and I eagerly wait it out. I think I've gone crazy writing books about you that I can shout. One minute away and you'll be mine.

Dystopian

The year is 2463, the events of 2020 is that of the past placed in a global history regents exam. I'm walking past the people that are broken and sad on the streets, making a living like they don't give a damn. It's the future of tomorrow and we are trapped because we owe Uncle Sam. I ignore the feelings of dismissal, rejection, and dejection from reality because I was never placed first or anybody's first choice so I have to compensate for loneliness with an artificial hologram. I pretend to come home to someone with a batch of roses in my hand to be excited to talk about how our day was, what we did, sit down and enjoy a basic meal and clinking glasses. I tell her to sit on my lap and it just feels so real and she cusps my soft face and stares in my tired eyes. An AI I bought to keep me company because my time is controlled like an hourglass. My job makes me cynical as I have to chase down people who don't have the same views as the Almighty Leader and it's disgusting what they do to them and I can't process emotionally what comes to pass. I've pulled the trigger each time and I feel a little more broken inside because it becomes easier and saying it to her I just feel like a jackass. She's an embodiment of everything I need and want and even gives me therapy and seemingly a friend nonetheless. That's when I saw her from my window in this tiny apartment, a girl getting soaked in the rain in this dark city looking back at me that somehow found my address. My information is supposed to be kept secret and my phone vibrates, a message saying to meet her outside and to come alone and to wear something to impress. I tried to leave but my AI trapped me, maybe it became jealous of my little date and was in distress. It strapped me in a chair and electrocuted me saying how everyone I ever tried to love only leaves me in the dust. It reminded me how I always had to second guess their intentions and wondered if their actions and words ever meant anything or if it was just lust. It's true of what she's saying and she has been the constant one and was there for me who lived through it all because it was an ancient conscious mind of my old memories that the old me created to remind me. I didn't care because I was still human after all and I must break free. Maybe she'll understand. Maybe not. I told her that I did love her because she will always be a part of me but I can't keep living this way as the job I have traumatizes me on a daily basis. She let's go and let me be. I met the mysterious girl who had a mission for me. Although she was forbidden for any men, she said she found a soulmate for me and wants to get rid of my sins and that nobody should have to kill or die anymore. I was inclined to believe her because my AI ran a quick background check. She wanted me to be careful and to keep an eye out but the mysterious girl with pink hair gave me a peck. It was like sweet poison and I wondered if she did all of this for attention, grabbing a sack to kidnap me. Strapped again to a chair, I was being interrogated and tortured. This is what it feels like to be vulnerable and to trust people again? This is a far cry. This is why I keep my distance from people and only trust myself and become self sufficient because this happens over and over. I don't even understand what this mysterious girl wants other than to hurt me over a generalization that all men are dogs and are the vermin of the earth. I've heard all of this before and one last request of my AI to help, since after all she is me, and she digitizes into a human body I thought I would never see again. She was strong and agile, efficiently getting rid of my attacker and gave peace to my brain. She kissed me and told me she will always keep me safe no matter what and said the mysterious girl was right, she did find a soulmate for me. I didn't know what she was referring to but she walked to a machine with the exact same body of my love from centuries ago and said that her programming was a conscious mind saved in a hard drive developed for this purpose. Before I can say anything, a blue light emerges from the machine and the woman opens her eyes, smiles at me with her sweet grin and runs to me. She's wet from the water and naked, but I didn't care. She just hugged me and held me there tightly. She told me she missed touching the real me and now we can be together forever. It seemed like a fairy tale ending but at this point I'll take anything to be happy with her eternally.

Little Boat in the Sea

All I wanted to do was take my little boat and paddle in the sea peacefully. All I did was mind my business and as I was moving on you hit me like a tidal wave and knocked me off drastically. You came back into my life after you blocked and left me. I regained my composure when you hyped it up and became distant but I have to remain balanced, that is the key. I get back on my little boat and dust myself off and attempt to enjoy the nice day but I remember we went out to eat and went for a drive down the highway but then I felt crappy. It felt as if I was being used and suddenly a little cloud manifested above me and rained on me but it felt warm like dog pee. I haven't heard from you for months but I guess that's okay because I haven't seen anybody. The sun hit brightly and the little cloud went away. I continued on my little venture and saw some dolphins and laughed at me maliciously. I wonder what they would do to me. They aimed their little hoses at me and blew water at me that knocked me on my rear and I hit my head on a corner. I had a little flashback of feeling warm and fuzzy with a girl but then it had to end abruptly because it wasn't right and I was sad but I had to endure the slaughter. The flashback turned into a bit of a horror. I randomly remembered a time when I took a girl out and it was going okay except she took too long to arrive, made my knees hurt as if I was an old man, and fluctuated between having a good time and being embarrassed half the time but I felt like an explorer. I did have fun but it was super awkward because I couldn't exactly be myself without having her judge me every so often. It ended with an awkward goodbye hug but I was willing to give it some more time but she put me in a coffin. Dry responses to none at all. This is what led me back to more thoughtful poses as a seagull came and ruined my thoughts with something disgusting. I wiped it off and tried to enjoy my trip on this little canoe, enjoying the sea breeze and the freedom and serenity found at sea. The weather was beautiful and warm and I tried my best to have a blast and tried to enjoy my iced tea. I looked to my left and a recycled paper bag covered my face for a second, blinding me as I panicked to get it off, almost crashing into rocks. The rocks and pebbles reminded me of a time when I had an insane crush on a blue eyed demon who was aloof and we went out to eat several times but I guess I didn't catch the tune that I was confused. I kept questioning if she really liked me or not because she kept taking me out week after week and I thought it meant something. I guess it wasn't much because she taught me that I'm way too trusting. After the fourth week there was no going back as she flew away to Mars to visit the earth a few years later as if nothing happened. The next was my own fault as I was confused again but the affections and playing around felt a bit real for me but I kept pouting. Nothing good came out of it as I became more annoyed at her actions and behavior. I rowed my boat back to the mainland but as I got to the port, I fell face first because I tripped on a traitor. The little boy laughed at me and ran away as he completed his wager. I tied a hard knot to keep my boat safe but then a drunkard on a yacht parked on the same spot and annihilated my little canoe. I didn't get as upset because I still have plenty of money but the captain gave me some more of it anyway. Sure, a little write off to a small debt as he laughed at the wooden pieces floating on the ocean. I continued off to sit down on a little table to enjoy some lunch with lemonade, looking cool with my aviators since I was sensitive to the light to an extent. They bring my shrimp and fries in a little container and before I take my first bite this entitled girl sits on my table and takes a bite out of my food, calling me cute. I sip my lemonade and wonder where she came from as I wanted to be alone but she was successful in seducing me momentarily as I became clumsy. We talked for a bit and she handed over her number in a piece of paper. She kissed me softly and departed but I was still hungry. I reminisced of a time where I was really close to having a girl of my own but my stupidity was greater than my logic and it happened twice. Once in the summertime in my early teens and clicked really well with a girl and we spoke day and night but I saw something I didn't like and got turned off and maybe it wasn't even there to begin with. I probably was tripping and hallucinated for a moment and honest to god I tried to go back but it wasn't the same. The other time I was talking with a girl who looked scary but I looked past that, almost securing a kiss but her charcoal aroma was killing me. Maybe I was too picky. Maybe I was an idiot but I was young and it was tricky. Riding a bike back to my hotel I realized I paid my dues for now. Staying on my lane this road ranger tried to slam into me because he says I took his girl. It was a police officer but a tad bit chunky. I don't know what he was talking about because she doesn't seem to be into him. He followed me back and I tried to remain calm but this was insane. The porter tried to hide me behind the curtain but obviously it wasn't a bright idea. The cop found me but I evaded and dodged his lame attacks as I rolled over and tripped him. I ran to my room and locked myself in. Maybe she's all I've got left and am lucky but the little misfortunes follow me endlessly. It isn't too late but now I heard on the news that we have to stay indoors for some time as these Godzilla-like creatures tear the city down and I can't leave my room unless I sneak around for food. This is taking too long and I wish it would resolve quickly because I want to see her.

Childish Anger

If I'm being honest I might be too nice. Nothing will ever suffice. Every time I try to seclude myself and meditate, people encourage me to open myself up and let it melt like ice. They reach out to me and pretend to get to catch up with me but their hidden agenda is to get help from me and it's like a vice. No matter how angry I am, I always run to help but I try to keep it concise. Everyone wants something from me and tests my patience. You don't have to butter me up because I've seen it coming from a mile away. Is this my final price? I understand there's a crisis going on and my first world problems won't make it any better and I'm so focused on my anger I can't see the world is burning. It's not just towards you but it's nearly everyone else, too. They cry about not having enough or that they get abandoned but they're not the only one because you've gone through it, too. Enough is enough. You never cared about quality friends, you have this urgent need of quantity. I'll help because I have to but I'll cut it short to protect you from my bipolarity. It's like they don't deserve me and I breathe in the hostility. It's nothing new because it remains the same, the inconsistency. I toss and turn to make peace with it but the poison runs strong in my veins and I want to go on a rampage viciously. I'm laying down looking at the ceiling trying to calm down but the animosity goes on. The curiosity to see the reactions and if it's my last apology. The childish anger that causes me to keep people at a distance and loving at arm's length, always mistrusting them because I hate being right. I'm a toxic being and I can taste the metal in my mouth and I want to write my own eulogy. I rather slam my tongue in a car door ten times than being vulnerable to you again. It's the little things that add up, little things that don't matter, little things I don't react to but I guess it's taking a toll now. Then I act like nothing is happening and I don't mind talking to you because I do but it boils my blood when it ends abruptly. It's not like I'm looking for an apology. I'll come to terms with it because it's human nature but would it be fair when you're nasty to me when I act the same towards you? I don't know and frankly I don't care anymore. I bid the tribute goodbye and I'll shower in my own childish tears of impotence and anger.

Time after Time

It came to me in a dream in a sense of déjá vu. I've gotten the letter that would send me to the military. I was in shock when I cracked the envelope open and it requested my intelligence and strength rapidly. I came to you in tears as I showed you the letter, telling you how badly I will miss you and laid a few kisses on your cheek that nobody else will see. I told you I don't know for how long it will be but I will do everything in my power to survive and come back for thee. One last hug and off to the bus I go. They cut my hair short and promoted me to lieutenant. I studied the strategies and battle plans and next thing I know I was on a plane off site. I went onward with my platoon and pushed towards the objectives. Everything was a blur because it was day in and day out. I wrote letters to you everyday to keep constant contact and never forget about you. I kept a picture of you tucked in a wallet of mine. The things I saw and went through are horrible. An explosion and a flying knife almost took my eye out. I survived it all but not all of my teammates, sadly. After 24 months the war was over. It has been a long time in this desert and I had no idea of what was going on back home. I spoke to my superiors and they finally let me go, a dutiful service for this country. My body isn't exactly the same as I took the train to school to go about my business. My hair has gotten longer and there's a scar on my right eye. You saw me and ran towards me as I picked you up, tightening our grips. You light the match and I set the fire. I remember you said you need excitement in your life and that's definitely me albeit the time you had to wait for me. You're tired of the same routine day in and day out but I'll be here to make it better. We can go and run on the beach as you push me towards the water playfully. The worst part is already done, I just want to spend my days with you.

Filtered Sadness

Big house all alone with the cloud sky hitting the windows just right. It's dark out even though it is way past day time, a dark oozing light. I remember the time we shared might have been special, hitting me with deep memories of July and September. I've been thinking again and the feelings hit me again mainly because I've pushed them back deeper. I know I moved on a bit but I still think of those old times that linger. Why do I still get jealous of little past memories? I already sacrificed some angels for you but it wasn't worth it, or it was, probably. Buying time for something I know that isn't for me and now we just act like strangers and nothing happened. It's not like I am entirely gloom but after these feelings pass because I've been struck by lightning again. I recovered some photos I tried to burn by putting my hand in the flames. Even though it hurts, I still smile at the little gifts of emotions you have given me. I was selfish the same and took back what I gave you yet you haven't noticed. It's okay because I'm trying to heal but those moments are still missed. Even though we weren't ever together, we always asked each other for kisses and to hear our voices that sent tingling sensations through our nervous system and it kept us focused. Sometimes it feels like we aren't really talking and sometimes the conversations can be dry and sometimes I wonder if we really are close anymore. The negative thoughts that creep up to me catch me off guard as I fight it off by holding on to the good we potentially had. I sometimes still feel hurt but it's fine, maybe you suffer during down time as well or maybe you don't. I still catch myself being a bit upset when you don't entirely read the letters I gave you but it's my childish anger getting the best of me. It's hard to take control of myself in times like these so I just have to keep pushing forward. I remember once upon a time you said we shared a powerful connection and missed me deeply but at times I wonder that since I'm here now if those thoughts and feelings remain the same. It's not reciprocated but that's okay, I may have found something better as far as I know but it doesn't hide the fact that at night sometimes it does kill me a little inside. It's okay, I'm stronger than I was before and it won't phase me as time goes on. It doesn't have to be all negative but I just hope you don't regret it and that it meant something, too. I don't understand what it is that got to me but seeing you again made me think back to a different time. Maybe it's part of the ten step process of grievance but I fear that one day you'll come back to me and that it'll be too late. You don't remember much of anything or you've pushed back the memories but sometimes I dislike it when you say you'll do something and then you don't and have a different version of the same memory. I wonder just how selfish and childish I am acting right now but these are my thoughts so I apologize in advance for them. Touching these walls that feel like water reminds me of something I could have had but it wasn't the right time or circumstance. It still burns me a bit when you take action on others and react to them when they aren't what you needed but maybe it's me being a toxic possessive monster. I'm always set aside and you kept saying how you rarely have a foundation but yet you were with them and saying how I'm the only support you had but I don't know if it's true yet I believed it at the time. The dark house will settle and shine bright tomorrow but for now let me enjoy this bitter sweet moment of sadness, a shade of weakness I have to let pass for tomorrow I will be better. I rather be alone but the torture of endless thoughts haunt me like a ghost.

Four Walls

I got cocky and it was just about two weeks since I've seen you and now I'm laying here wishing that I actually hugged you as hard as I possibly could. Stuck in these four walls and lord knows when I will see you again but I know the feeling will be good. For now I'm just remembering you dancing around with your dirty white converses and I smiled sheepishly at you. I didn't know how to act other than hiding it to keep things professional but I know you can tell from your point of view. You grew on me, haven't you? You didn't make me laugh as much as I make you but it's okay but I'm always staring at you as much as I stare into blank space. I remember the time everybody kept asking me if I gave you your treasured gift yet but events kept popping as a bad kid's bop CD until I finally found the perfect opportunity where nobody would ruin it. I keep repeating the same memory over at times but I can't forget you doing a cute little squeal and your feet moving like a girl who jumps rope playing hopscotch. You were cheesing so hard and your grin had me weak but my overconfident demeanor made me feel in control and remained suave. You read the little words on the cover and the back and was so excited for the random gesture. At the end you thanked me again and reached for a brief yet tight suffocating hug I love. Now I'm kicking rocks at home and cheering when you ask me for help as I reread some of the jokes I made and replay the voice messages. Your voice is calming like the sounds of the oceanic waves I wish we were on, holding hands and kissing passionately. This cursed virus makes it harder for things to naturally flow and prolong it, and yes, I know it's not a big deal because there are other more important things going on in this world. I always have bad timing with things and it's not quite fair with such circumstances but maybe this will be the most hopeful thing I have ever had the pleasure of having since 2018. I sing and dance in the shower, making sure I don't slip and fall, and messing around with my hair while making faces in the mirror pretending we are starring in a 50s movie. Your beauty is something so natural because you don't need makeup to highlight your features and even though I act goofy, things still run smoothly between us. I don't know what it is but whatever I say or do doesn't bother you as much and even at the most horrible things I say, which I apologize for internally with a major facepalm, but maybe when we return there is something to discuss. I remember the day when you were acting silly in the morning speaking in a British accent that gave me a light bulb in my mind that gave more of a plus. I think the narcissism in me that makes me see you as a constant reminder of me that makes me like you more, and no, it's not just because of our shared qualities but more of how scary it is. I still cannot get over at how we think and act the same way at times and I must be an idiot to choose others over you. The compulsion and impulses of speaking my mind outright towards you as you chuckle especially at things that aren't even funny at all keeps me puzzled day in and day out. If only we can take a trip to Mars and spend a week together somehow but instead I'm pouting.

Dark Anger

Why am I still so angry for some of the times I think about you? Why can't I let it go like I did before? It's not so hard but I still harbor immature feelings. It's worse than Bruce Wayne not letting it go, he can't let go, the death of his parents. I'm not a victim because I did damage, too. Maybe it's the fact that I'm stuck in prison paying for a crime I didn't commit, boo hoo. I toss and turn at night, have to keep an eye out because I have no crew. I'm screwed up mentally, the cold fall day I checked my phone the day you left and the cops were closing in and the moments I had were few. I was handcuffed for you, I knew where you hid the body and how deep the grave you made. I'm always on guard yet I'm still vulnerable to it but I still get played. I'm not meaning to throw some shade. I'm just still appalled to it, to everything but it's hard to let go and there's nothing to do but to evade it in my mind. The warden keeps an eye out but for how long before he gets bought and preyed on. I kept you on the visitors list but you didn't bother to show up, not even with an alias or a disguise and left me to rot and I have to accept you're gone. I bop my head to the music replaying in my head to tire myself out emotionally and cheer up by watching Spider-Man but after the show ends, the endless thoughts are there and it's like a magnet, I'm drawn to it. I wake up early at dawn. I'm ill and I speak in a low tone, coughing up madness and I feel like a moron. Don't excuse yourself out now, this was our fault but maybe more of my own. It's a jungle out here while you're spending the money lavishly and sleeping without a growing conscience. I don't know why I decided to protect you but I'm used to it, I guess. I looked at the judge as he sentenced me 25 to life and now I'm here while you might be planning your wedding as you looked beautiful in your dress. It's worth punching the wall in a little fit but I trained myself to calm down. I was a stupid little kid but that was five years ago and I have twenty more to go. It doesn't matter if I get out on good behavior because I feel so slow in this, you ruined the flow. I'll find peace in the next decade and solace after that but this will be tough to get through.

Is Love Real?

I'm sorry you feel that way, that you don't believe in love yet you had a significant other before and said that they meant the world to you. How can you say love doesn't exist if you told them you love them? How can you feel guilty of what you did if love isn't real? You've had a few bad relationships but mostly they were trash and losers. They weren't self sufficient or men enough to actually make you safe or feel that they were all you needed. They didn't nurture you and they took you for granted. You did everything for them but they didn't bat an eye. Now, thanks to them, you believe you're broken but it's more of a headache than anything. You only see the world in black and white, there is no grey area. They probably never loved you in the first place and you didn't deserve that. Now, thanks to them you hate everyone now and I wonder if I ever made that list. I'm not as stuck as I once was and it's not a slap on the wrist anymore. You say you want to do better but you don't act on it and don't put the work in, expecting change without effort. Now I'm making the same mistake giving my energy and attention to people that might not deserve, or maybe they do, because it's not like I'm hoping you to care about me anymore but you need some light in your life because all you see is the plain negativity. It sucks feeling that way, a hole you can't seem to climb out of but it's no longer my problem to an extent but you don't help yourself do better. It's a hard world out there but we, as humans, have to put in the work or maybe it's a persistent problem I yet do not understand. You complain about certain things and not reaching goals that you always wanted to do but you sit there waiting for some things to fall on your lap. I have offered myself in vain to you but it's okay, the heart wants what it wants. It's not like I'm walking away entirely like you have done me but it'll be a little break I owe to myself. The stupidest reasons for them to leave you over something they were weak and not good enough for them to take care of themselves, having to control you. You say that some just let you be yet didn't give you enough attention since you came knocking on my door and I stupidly opened it eagerly. Maybe this was doomed from the start and I've just opened my eyes because I was sleeping on it. There's no shade in it, it is just my truth, and if you see this I am truly sorry. Is love real? It is for me. It makes you want to wake up in the morning, it makes you want to do better. Loving yourself first and foremost is what's important to be able to love someone. You need internal peace before you can find happiness externally so if and when it ever goes, you'll be okay. I've been shut out numerous times before and this might be too tiring to stay on this path. Love for me is what gives hope for a tomorrow but not betting all my chips on the table because I have to take care of myself first. At the same time as opposing as it sounds, love is what makes you want to have faith in people again to not be scared of what tomorrow brings. Loving deeply, loyally, fondly and having butterflies in my stomach when I see their message can be seen superficial but maybe it's this idealistic view that is the meaning that is true for me. I've never experienced it to a real degree but this is what I imagine it to be. Sadly, you never had any real love to begin with so maybe that's why you say love isn't real. It's okay. One day you'll see and maybe if it isn't with me, maybe someday you will, unless I am the best you'll ever get while everyone else is a downgrade. I don't know what the future holds but whoever I'm lucky to find who will love me back after centuries of living, I'll hold them deeply and they will know what true love is. They don't have to look over their shoulder or be paranoid with whom I'm speaking to or texting. They'll wake up every morning without feeling empty, with them feeling that absolutely nothing is missing and nothing needed elsewhere. Maybe I say that now but I have to hold it to myself to keep it truer than death. An idealistic boy who has lived longer than the world has spun its first day. Maybe someone will be as lucky as me. You'll see. Whoever ends up being with me will get everything they wanted, everything they ever wished for, everything they ever hoped for and have a sensation further beyond completeness.

Selfish

I cry and whine and act like a victim when I might be the one hurting people. My toxicity is lethal. I try to change for the better but I keep acting territorial. I know I have to pay for my dues and whatever that is coming to me is what I deserve because what I have done is illegal. I sit back and remember a slightly embarrassing moment where the young ones say I am a chick magnet, highly social with messages from unsaved numbers. Putting me on the spot I just left quickly and pretended not to hear as they got louder and louder. I wanted to hide away as they grew in loud numbers with their power. You said that it means nothing with a straight face and I wonder if you felt anything inside. I didn't bring it up but I wonder if you also think I'm a jerk, a player, an abuser and a user. One of the young ones felt bad for me and shook his head as he knew I liked you and had it really bad. I knocked it off and pretended I didn't know what was going on as we both smiled at each other, a smiley face grin showing off our pearly whites. Now I'm locked up and can leave this man made box every forty eight hours but it's alright. I can only dance to the beat on my own and imagine little scenarios in my head that give me such powerful insights. I replay little moments in my mind and pretend I'm watching a Netflix series while sipping on Sprite. I long for this whole thing to be over so I can pretend to be suave and feel your strong arms around my back again and this time I will hold you and not be as gentle as I usually am, squeezing you tight. God, I miss you and I think I'm crazy for thinking about you and not being able to sleep till way past midnight. I think I have symptoms but I know you'll cure me, right?

The Gift

You did your hair beautifully and got the t-shirt that mirrored the little present I got for you. Did I actually inspire you? They ask me what qualities I look for in a woman and honestly I don't know. I just want someone to be down for me and who actually cares for me. I just know that if her personality matches with mine, however she may be, that is what matters most. I don't care if she's taller or shorter, if she's blonde or not, black or white, whatever, I just want someone to say a sweet toast with. They say I'm a healer and attract people who are unloved and need help because my foundation is set like a monolith. You seem to be alright, strong mentally but I still don't know you personally. I'm doing all I can while keeping a distance because I don't want to scare you away. A little insider, I'm thinking if that's what it is, the red t-shirt of the young little wizard the day right after I gave you the enchanted journal. Did you truly wear that on purpose or was it a coincidence? Nobody believes in coincidences but it was the following day I gave you the book and I love your childish innocence. If only I can read your mind but it's an invasion of privacy and I know you keep your cards close to your chest. I love it when you say I'm the best because it makes me grin and feel impressed. The leather of the book with a fancy ribbon that tightens the book with special designs and you just got so happy and you seemed to pass my little test. Now my not so discreet messages makes me wonder if I messed up because my heart is always worn on my sleeve and I just don't want to end up alone or die alone, as if my feelings were repressed. I just don't care anymore and want to let it go and just be with you, happily ever after.

Your Looks

I've been preying on your soul since I walked in that room on that hot summer day. The first thing I noticed was your tattoo of wings on it as I was sweating and tired from the fire in me, stuttering trying to say my name. I didn't notice it at first but I loved the way your eyes shrunk as your smile overshadowed it and I felt the flame. I kept staring at you discreetly and laid my eyes on your toned skin that traced your shapely legs as I looked down at the paper, smiling and pretending it's a game. I've studied the way your lips are shaped to your dimples when you smile and I try to imitate the sound of your voice the way I hear it in my brain. Just a lost little boy with a crush as I stare at your frame. You're slim and short sized that packs a lot of influence on me. I want to caress your hair and play with it, staring at your eyes as I say the right things that make you blush a bright red making magic that's carefree. I want to press my lips and trace the anatomy of your arms, your hands, fingers all the way down to your knee. If only we can interlock our hands together, feeling your blood pump through your veins as I hear your heartbeat tense up and increase rapidly. I want to hear you gasp as my soft and gentle kisses on your neck catches you by surprise. I want to have you gazing at me with lust and wonder through your snake eyes. You can whisper subtle and dirty things to my ear as you analyze my body language and seduce me to my demise. You're not just the grand prize, you just might be my sun rise. Your fingers can stroke my long hair and pull out my grey ones as you laugh at me for nibbling your ear with delicate love bites. Your hands rub on my chest and feel my tense, developed shoulders as you give me a little fright. You can boss me around and you slip my sweater out of me as you hungrily stare just for a second as I look down shyly with a smirk,holding up my chin to meet your sight. You let me rip open your shirt as you claw at my chest and let your appetite roam freely. Close down the blinds so we can enjoy this out of sight.

Come and Go

It's been a long war and I've finally come back. I see people come and go and it's easier being accustomed to it, having nothing to lack. It still is a challenge when you let people in and when they trust you with their deepest and darkest of secrets it becomes a knack. I come and go because I don't stay around for much because I don't have a specific pack. I drift around with no end place in mind with no end goal. I make connections everywhere that seem deep at first and when I'm gone, it feels like there's a hole in my life but I learn from it to become whole. The depth of the intimacy with people I am privy to know of makes me miss them but it's nothing compared to what I stole. They're like nobody I have ever met and it's hard to come by when I meet new people. It's a harsh reality when you learn things about yourself that you never knew you had in the first place. There's not enough space in my memory to hold the lessons I've learned from them and it leaves fast like a race. You may become codependent on them because you've opened up to them as they did to you in levels not everyone gets to that isn't available in any marketplace. It's okay because one of us will leave without a trace. You think about them from time to time but there's nothing much that can be done and you search them up to reshuffle the memories and moments in your inner interface. There have been a few constants in my life and in the short moments they were gone it took me a long time to train myself to let go and feel used to it. It's hard not being able to share things like good news or jokes when they're gone, isn't it? Eventually this is part of growing up when you realize things will have to end to start anew and you must submit. You'll have to split it all in half and recommit to a stronger you. If you aren't authentic to it all then it'll just be a waste of time and a counterfeit. Just go with the flow and the only way is forward.

4:44

There are many things I have wished for during these odd hours in my life.
I have wished for them, for you, for me and I wondered if they have ever
wished anything for me or of me, and I have no idea who she would be, my
future wife. I think often and try to keep busy but nothing seems to work
and I slowly become paranoid. Sometimes I keep up an act as if I was an
android. I promise I'm not using my good looks to get my way or to fill my
void. I'm as human as any other despite my evil antics, my devilish
charms, my childish sense of humor and my emotional ways that are
always extreme but I control it well in my subconscious like the theories
Freud. It's hard dealing with racing thoughts of you and whether good or
bad, salty or not, I still dream of you and even I get annoyed. It's worse
than the lows of a steroid. I hold onto the memories of your grin and the
sounds of your laughter. I can't get you out of my mind and your name is
always on my lips even after I die tonight. I can't deny it or lie to myself, I
sensed the vibes that caused me a longing delight I haven't felt for months
on end. Ever since November you crept on my mind faster than you did in
July. When I was down in December you kept me from straying to an
endless pit and it was hard saying goodbye. I'm a bad guy because I get
tangled in all these events and my little fits just don't apply. I wrote about
you many times and I loved it when you asked me what happened to my
scratched eye. I smiled like a little boy, eager to tell you a funny version of
you and you laughed a little bit too loud in a quiet room and you let me
have a piece of your special pie. I know we don't know each other too well
but my gut feelings cannot betray. Everybody says so and makes such a big
deal no matter how hard I laugh about it and lead myself astray in disarray.
I find other people to prove the opposite but when it comes down to it, I
am backed up by a sea of people who want to manifest something magical
beyond Broadway. I promise you I'm trying to fall back because I feel as
though I'm bothering you but every Steve Trevor needs his
WonderWoman. It doesn't matter how hard I push you away mentally,
emotionally I am a magnet to you and with everything my two little
helpers tell me gives me nothing but positive remarks, surely there must be
a plan. I brood like Batman because life is literally on hold as I'm stuck on
my mind without any action as things slow down and decrease like my

lifespan. 4:44, I make every wish like I did before but now I have to spread my wings and soar.

Stuck Mentally

I find myself finding out things about myself that puts me down but I build myself up. The shades of sadness transform from discords but I'm trying to stay sane by drinking from this cup. You have an idea but you can't destroy it even if you kill the person. You can't destroy the idea and it is contagious that can help you build yourself up or destroy you because an idea is resilient. I dream about you but when I wake up you're not there. I try to destroy so I can become the opposite of what I am but at the end of the day I am a healer. I can do that just by making you laugh, with my presence or with just my words. I burn myself with a cigarette because it's ten again. I have to make sure the days actually pass by or else I'm living in a reaper limbo in a loop I'm trying to break from the chains. I vibe with myself mainly because not many people can match my energy because they can say all they want I'm cute but I take L's as if it was a sport and I have to hop off this train. I'm stuck in my head and paranoid because I'm above outer space while the mortals play baseball with people who act like gems and diamonds but turn out to be a bunch of bronze valued personalities. Not everyone is on my level and I'm trying so hard not to come off aggressively because my brutality is a monstrous fatality. Don't get your hopes up they said, don't fantasize they said, but it's hard to do so when the actions measure up far beyond words but maybe it's betrayal all over again as I sit back and think critically. Calm down because this will be worth something in its totality.

Live Forever

Waking up in the jungle with the temperatures rising so high you can see the mist of heat. I beat my chest as if I was a monkey or gorilla boasting my superiority as I recall a bloody night full of violence and ferocity as if I was a savage dog on the street. My hands are sticky and warm but my face feels cold with a nervous shock as my legs tremble yet I slept like a baby and don't know what happened next as my memory becomes obsolete. I don't know what purpose I served for but the vague flash backs serve as a constant reminder that I served a lord to do his bidding. My backs hurt as if my wings were yanked off but it is a sensation of familiarity. How did I know I had wings? Wasn't I but a man who enjoyed a life of luxury with his materialistic things? I look at myself at the river and I see small scars of bullet holes that are still healing slowly as the jewels on my wrists remind me of a time where the relics of the past still existed, the ancient kings. A reflection of a tired young man yet I feel battered and old, bones cracking as if I were an elder but my limbs still strong. Forever and ever just living for years to come as I remember more and more. The evil awakening I promised myself to seal away as I stuck my finger to the gods above only to strike lightning at me. Laughing it off they knew it wasn't enough for me to continue my little rebellion against them. You loved them more than me, huh? It was painful to force my wings to grow back but I did it anyway, I retracted my wings out that were shades of burgundy as the blood was still fresh on them. I bellowed out a savage cry as it hurt like hell. A fallen angel that was cast out due to vanity and jealousy, a self esteem way too high with a confidence that marked the bear on my smile. No, I am not Morningstar but I,too, am in style. I won't tempt people as much but my very existence is a temptation as I slowly change people to think and act like me. There is no need for any more destruction. There is no more revenge I want to take, I'll throw it all away because it's too tiring because I have a new instruction. A new plan I set for myself and I will complete it in my own fashion, a seduction. I'll embrace my darkness but at the same time I'll be your light you never knew you needed. I'll make myself be your favorite and you'll want me back even after I walk away. It'll be an endless torture until I come back, begging to have me because you can't replace me, find anybody like me and wouldn't know what to do without me and imagining a life in my absence is devasting. You'll enjoy my childish ways, you'll enjoy my goofy laughter, and you'll miss me for I will be in your thoughts day in and day out. I'll pretend but be genuine at once, holding back while my heart is worn on my sleeve. You'll never meet or know anyone like me and you will not want me to leave. It doesn't matter how long it takes, I'll be here forever. Nobody can tell you otherwise because I'll be a special someone for you even if it doesn't feel the same. The endless torture of being an immortal won't be lame. You'll love me hopefully but if you take too long who will be to blame?

Dark Moods

My heart is pounding heavily. My fists are clenching that suppresses a destructive possibility. I turn on the music louder to have something to bop. The bass feeds the dopamines and feelings I've been trying to stop. The sunglasses I have on still can't hide the stress and white rage that can be described as leaving something in the sunlight for just a bit and it lights up in flames. Holding the venom inside me I have to control and tame myself because this is just a child's game. The mind games, the confusion, not knowing, it's all putting me in a foul mood only I have power in changing and I can't even remember my own name. I have to go far out in full speed to make sure there is no collateral damage. From a slow jog to a sprint where it seems to compete with the Flash, I have to find a solid and solitary place to explode but it's a challenge. Judgemental and critical of others, I easily point out what's wrong with people but I can't exactly place what they're good at. It's driving me insane because I feel like such a jackass but I know I'm right. I'm not a doormat. I know I'll fall flat because I can't control the contents of my own mouth as it lays piercing words that stab like a sword and chop cleaner than a guillotine. Why can't I be normal but I don't want to be, and I don't want to hear it, but I know I can be mean. I've been trying to regulate my behavior but it's just so sweet to unleash the load with hormones raging more than a teen. I can't be scared of the obstacles or consequences because I'm insane without much remorse as it is unusually satisfying living fearlessly with energy as if I was high on caffeine. Two hours away from the city with millions of miles between us I can rage peacefully. I can thrash around and break the mountains apart, kicking down trees as I let out a gruesome yell. I dare someone to challenge me. I want someone to. Animal cruelty? Me? But how could it be? A gigantic overlord of a grizzle comes charging at me and wants to take a crack at me. I try to avoid hurting it entirely. I don't know what happened next but I was standing on top of it with my fat resting on its back. Victory? How, tell me, really? I feel a bit bad but maybe this little wolf inside me needed some fresh air as the feelings simmer down. I climb over the rubble of the pieces of mountain as I let out a dragon like roar with flames shooting out.

Space Odyssey

An astronaut from 1993. I've taken quarantine since then because I was sucked in by a blackhole and even though I'm 23, my scanners say it's 2020. I've traveled through time in an instant but it didn't feel that way. I've been in isolation for so long I've prayed to die. My logic was stronger than my reoccurring thoughts and hopelessness. I wanted to go back home but the space station I was armed with no longer exists. How can I reach the people I loved for so long and now would they even recognize me? Did they bury an empty casket and do they miss me? Perhaps they have forgotten me. I survived on water and MREs. Jesus, it's so beautiful out here but living in the dark for so long as I touch the cold glass, staring at the stars making a wish every time as I look to the right towards Mars. Have you forsaken me, oh wise one? A little mission to explore past the heavens was a sign of vanity but no man had been punished for doing so. Special storms that scared me into a corner as I saw strange colored flames and thunderstorms rage past my shuttle saddle away from me. Maybe I've been hallucinating and dreaming. Maybe this isn't real yet my face remains young. My body adjusts to the tremors of fright as my survival instincts kept me safe for months. I saw things you wouldn't believe fly past me. There's life outside ours but nobody would believe me. What lurks in the shadows? An alien approached me and looked exactly like me. He spoke in a strange language and told me I was his clone but I knew damn well I was born on Earth. Has he been stalking me privately? He takes my hand and I feel a sensation of joy yet I'm scared. He shares his memories with me of an insomniac wandering around and promised to take me back home but the Earth is not ready just yet. He told me he'll take me back by the end of April because the disease will kill me if I go back now. What future lies ahead?

Her Voice

It's the most soothing thing I have heard in a long while even though I live by the ocean. It's quite calming in my little castle where I hear the seagulls chirp and the waves crashing against one another and her lovely voice brings such strong emotion. I play the messages over and over just to remember the feelings I get that distorts the mental commotion. I love how your accent sounds and how you say my name, how it rhymes with brawn.

I gave you a little surprise and you seemed to love it as I tried to mentally record your little squeal and cheer of excitement. I tried to memorize the excited pitch in your voice that heightened. Your voice can calm down the inner storm inside me, setting up the playful violins that play with a soft piano tune. I've tried to resist your ways but I'm not immune. I want to call you just to check up on you and hear your voice. We can hold hands and rejoice because you're going to be my first choice. You keep my demons at bay. You bend my will like no other in months and once again I'm ready to betray. I'll let them burn just so I can have you and be with you. Crazy? Indeed. If I take off my mask and reveal the truest parts of me, would you want to carry my seed? Would you be able to handle the imperfections of mine and keep up with my speed? I have done many horrible things but for you I will bleed. The voice of yours is what keeps me glued together even though I'm perfectly capable of doing that on my own but you keep me in the zone. All I need to do is walk through the flames, past the floor of glass, through the mountains and past the oceans to hear you speak, saying literally anything with your sweet southern like accent with a drawl that can be understood everywhere yet misunderstood pronunciations. I have this sword right here and I'm ready to use however you wish it to be because I can destroy or build a nation for you. Why would I be devoted to you? The main reason is you're a reincarnation of me. You're my shield, I'm your sword. If you're the prophesized Amazon queen from eons ago I am ready to upgrade myself from slave to lover, from right hand to putting a ring on your finger. It doesn't matter now but I must fall back just a bit longer. This disease of mine has to be temperamental because your voice keeps me in this bubble. Your laughter reminds me to stay out of trouble. Should you banish me I know I'll be fine because I know now I have a double. Maybe not in this lifetime but eventually we will meet again.

Last Breath

Not sure what exactly to say. I'm on my last dying breath and the sky is turning grey. There's a gaping hole in my chest, a mortal wound that pierced my heart. My rifle beside me, the worst days I have seen since my platoon launched the speed boat. My brothers in green have been taken from me and now it's my turn and I hope you get the letters I wrote. I close my eyes and remember your sweet and delicate face where I can feel the warmth in my hands. I cherish that face with an unspoken truth and as I lay dying here I do not know how you feel and I wished I outlived these lands. I wanted to surprise you with a batch of flowers with my devilish smile and flicker my eyes at you. I wanted the wholesome feeling I have missed as I fought in this First World War and there is still so much I still want to do. I can't even dig this bullet out because a delicate mishap will be the end of me. I just want to lay here, look at the clouds and find your face in them, your chinky eyes that shrink when you smile or laugh. I want to see your soul, I want to hear the music you play when you dance and groove to the music blissfully and gracefully except I can't. Coughing up blood that lands on my jacket is not a good sign. I wish I had more time and this wound is not benign. Damn, if only I could have survived a bit longer to go back home to finally kiss your sweet, thick and moist lips. I could just hold your little hands and lock them into a fist with mine because nothing will break us. I am not ready to die and I know I'm the right guy. We might be destiny but all I can do now is cry. I can just hear you calling out my name in your accent, your voice, the sounds that makes my heart pounce with every whisper, hushed tones and anxious worry. Do you feel that? It's the butterflies in my tummy. I might have just fallen in love with you. Goodbye.

Teenage Angst

Being stuck for so long I have gone crazy and reverted to my overbearing and overemotional younger self again. I'm trying my best to shake it off but I find myself getting annoyed at the littlest of things and it hurts my brain. I overthink too much and find myself whining and chronically complaining in my mind over the smallest of things. It is mental torture of what the worries bring. We are all stuck together and have to wait it out but when the conversations run dry and the waiting makes me anxious for hours on end it's like I don't know them anymore. It's nothing like the past and the people we used to be and what I admired about them for now becomes a bore. I'm trying to meditate and make sense of all this but I get annoyed at how little effort I see. I expect too much from people because I tend to give my all but I know I do it because I want the same thing back and it's like nothing is enough because I'm spoiled and lucky. I want what I want when I want it because for a long time I had it that way for others wanting for so long to receive it back tenfold because I thought it was what I deserved. Teenage angst that came from a hellish past makes me want to scream and rip my hair out because it is so stupid because I know what it's like to get constantly curved. Juggling things to keep my mind busy and from becoming sad, I tell myself to get over myself from these first word problems because there's plenty of others living in abuse, unable to eat and dying on the inside every single day. Smacking literal sense into me only makes it temporarily better but then I try to focus my thoughts on you and in my mind I get my way. Suddenly I get shocked with a few jolts of electricity because it hits me how much I miss you and want to hear you. I move on from one unrequited to the next again and again but this time I'm hoping it's different because at the end of the day, no matter how many wars I've been through, how many golden cities I see rise and fall, how many ancient things have come and gone from extinction I'm still a little boy looking at this view. I am outside looking in always. I wanted to be the shiny object everyone wants to have as if I were a little child to be appraised. It's dramatic and childish but sometimes it feels like I never have seen to get it with my selfish ways and using tears to manipulate. It was easy to do so and won every time like in chess, checkmate. Too many versions of myself I'm pushing against like cattle in a meat locker with scars on the inside to pull myself together. I have to focus my energy on you and everything nice that would be because now you're my treasure. I know I can come across as lunatic and egotistic but my feelings are truer that any deity revealing themselves to mankind, worth way more than the broken gold standard of the United States, promising more than Gospels and verses. My disgusting highs and lows are hidden from the outside but it twirls inside like a hurricane and shatters me more than a level 10 earthquake as the devil in me curses. Two sides to one story as they say, two faces behind a mask, a legion of emotions running through me with a tired soul destroying a weight off his shoulders. It's like my mind and intense sentiments are asymptotic, never reaching a common ground as I'm split in two wanting different things. Vibing with myself I have to be okay and let things rock, never telling anybody anything, really, unintentionally I will do so due to my childish need for constant attention. I have reached a new point of being demented, I have to handle this tension and just blast off to another dimension, leaving people alone from my extremities. I wish not to bother anyone with my teenage angst.

It's Not Me

Centuries ago I remember someone close to me. I'm fighting a rich man's
war and the lasers almost burn my skin like acid as I sit behind this
gigantic blue tree. She was pretty much my first and it's uneasy to not feel
attached and the beautiful memories that I hold greedily, closely and replay
them mentally. The damage done isn't nearly as much as I've dealt against
countless others. My battle suit weighs heavy on me, too tired to continue
fighting but I'm the general and they need me so I can bring the soldiers to
their mothers and fathers. The dopamines I had let me love every part of
you, physically, emotionally and spiritually because back then I
worshipped you. Now I'm left a bit sad every now and then when the
memories creep back. The best friend I never knew I had was always there
to help me out and even when I'm ungrateful I was surprised tremendously
and needed an ice pack. I tried to get in your head to understand you and
other times I would find myself getting angry for things that happened way
back when and had nothing to do with me. Someone tried to sneak on me
but my reflexes shot up like a cat and I shot my enemy faster than John
Wayne on a quick draw. Leaning back, I try to hold back my tears behind
this dark bulky helmet and didn't even say thank you, such a shameful
flaw. Back when I was younger I was eager to help and happy you turned
to me but now I'm forgetting what it's like before I changed drastically.
Focusing my eyesight upgrades, I pick down the enemies from meters
away. Down they go one by one as my forces advance a few steps at a time
slowly winning this campaign. I'm just so sorry for the hurt and pain and
the piercing words that cut quicker than water entering a membrane. I still
can't shake it off because nobody gave me what you did previously and
those that came next just weren't the same, it didn't fill that empty void
when I was complete with you just for a little while. Reloading the
magazine I remember feeling left out so many times when I used to have
the constant affection but it was time to move on. Clicking back the rifle, I
zeroed in on my mission and tried my best not to zone out again but for
some reason I keep thinking of you, someone of my past I buried deep long
ago. I chuckled to myself at this little phenomenon. I was the first you
seemed to like that wasn't your type, especially admiring my brawn as I
said that there was something magical about you that I cherished as well,

even if you weren't my type either. I don't know, I guess I never believed in having a type because I like what I like and that's what came to mind when I first met you. Instantly attracted but I held back because you were miles away and I didn't think it was possible. I still appreciate everything you have done for me and even though you're gone now I remember your sweet smile and attractive voice you were self conscious about but I liked what I saw and heard. It's sad to say my immortality let me outlive you but the man you see today might put fear in you and probably be ashamed. Maybe if you were here now you would still accept all of me while I didn't do the same but kept trying because I am too harsh in judging you. I'm sorry. A few hours later, we won another victory of conquering this planet and ready to fly out into orbit for another conquest. I guess I just wanted to stay thank you and excuse my behavior despite everything, toxic or not, you are one of the few people from my past I feel close to even when it doesn't feel that way. As the spaceship travels across the millions of shooting stars and galaxies, I wish for you and pray that you're alright, wherever your soul may rest. I'm sure it's way above the heavens and you're happily playing with your pets of all kinds with your big animal loving heart. I remove my helmet and I see the scar on my eye, my cheeks that haven't healed just yet. My eyes have different color irises and my hair is grey, something I haven't seen in a long time. Maybe it's one of those special chemicals injected into me to look the part, as I'm a double spy collecting information and infiltrating the world governments. I place two fingers on my lips and place it on the window and think of you. Thank you. Just watch over me as I complete my mission and the future betrayals I am about to do. Pray for my soul, red siren.

That's What You Said

Sitting down and working, minding my own business, you were happy when I told you I was done with your work. I was giddy that I impressed you and finished the workload quickly and I gave you a little smirk. Thankful for my help, you said that's why you love me. At the moment I stayed quiet without saying anything because I was deep in thought on a Thursday. My heart is yours. Here, take it. I'll remove it from my chest and give it to you. It's yours. I love you, too. Now after serving my time, I want to act aloof and cool. When I see you, I want to give you the warmest smile I ever gave anyone and hope you tell me how much you've missed me as I stare into your hazel eyes that look like jewels. I'll lean against the wall, grab your fingers and stare in your eyes and say how I thought of you every minute and wondered how you were doing this whole time. You'll smile at me, biting your lip but maintaining composure. I give up and pull you in to me, holding you strongly and squeezing you so good that you have no choice but to crush my upper back like you always do. We'll be there for what seems like an eternity but in reality for a few seconds. It'll feel nice resting our tired young faces on each other's shoulders. Our little foundation will be built and last longer than it took to create boulders. You'll sneak a quick kiss on my cheek as I gently squeeze your arm before I go, running my fi gets through my hair. Smiling, we'll leave to our own rooms and be distracted and thinking about how we are little snacks. The longest hour ever until I see you again. Walking joyfully to your place, you look my way with a cheerful smile with a high energy I sense from you. I can feel my ears go warm as I play it off by showing my dimples I let only a few see. I steal a subtle touch on your arm and ask you if you want or need anything. With your face beaming, you say everything you need is right here.

Time

If I didn't know your name, you'd still be hot stuff. The waiting is putting a strain on me and it's tough. I heard they said we can't come back until the end of the year and it makes me angry. Everyday without speaking to you or knowing how you are is making me cranky. It's as if the gods are delaying my chances of being with you, seeing you, touching you. They cancelled the spring, canceled the last week of winter and I'll be damned if they cancel the summer. This is beyond a bummer. How much more of this do I have to wait? Who busted open the gates of hell? Who do I have to kill just to see you? I look at my watch and it doesn't make time go by any faster. I have to argue and convince the masters of chance and I'll curse the day in rage even when it's past Easter. My insides are twisting as if I were an addict, I need you, I want you, I want to hear you and speak to you. I'm pulling back because I don't want to bother you and it's hard as if I was playing hard to get but I'm truly not. I'm not sure how to deal with this situation we are in and the boundaries I ought to respect and draw the lines.

Stuck between these four walls and the invisible war being fought and you're only a phone call away or are you, really? I'm torn because I want to show initiative but the invasion of my presence might be unnecessary. I want to talk to you but you're too busy. You might just brush it aside again and it hurts my ego. I don't know what to do. I get blue. I just wish this was all over to seduce you with my charms in person, flicker a golden boy smile at you and be near you, our shoulders brushing and you not minding my soft, gentle touch. I miss you very much. I miss you so much it hurts. You're a superstar in your own right and you praise me back and when I stare at you, I subtly lick my lips because you look like dessert. We both are adults but playing this cat and mouse game to do our best not to be inappropriate and keep our salaries safe. It might be a mistake if we take too long but the little chase just makes it exciting. It's the little moments where it takes a smart one to read between the lines with silent affections that makes my heart beat faster. I can't hold it together and let out a wistful smile, a long sigh and react emotionally because you make it better. I want to run up to you and carry you in a powerful embrace without a care in the world and hoping you'd wrap your legs on me because you're just as happy. Wishful thinking and longing waits and this takes way too long, sadly. You've been on my mind a thousand times, constantly thinking about you and wished I dreamt about you more. It's open for you, my vulnerability for you, all the doors. I can lay my head on your pillow and just feel the tender sweetness and fall asleep with your smile being the last thing I see. Time is all I need but want it to go faster and when I finally see you for real my mind will say "yippee!".

Knots in my Throat

Is it okay? Why can't I react emotionally? Will I get punished? Can I express myself honestly or are you going to let me vanish? Can I get the same attention you gave them? Why is it that you can do whatever you want but when I do it I have to atone for it without a hum? Is it because I'm a megalomaniac and low key evil? Do I like being this way? Sometimes I do, sometimes I don't, I can't help what I feel and it's the real me under a defense mechanism but you want us to be equal? Is there an exception to our behavior? Why do you come to me when you know the bizzare things that come out of my mouth or is it because you really trust me and I am supposed to be a temporary savior? I am helpful, I can be kind, I can be an innocent little boy at times but with my misbehavior...it confuses what and who I really am. I've always been told I will struggle internally with my inherent nature but why must I be equally as malevolent as I am tender hearted? Does it feel good to get a good laugh when my edgy jokes push the limit of messed up things? Can I really say I have redeemable qualities? Am I what people expect me to be or do I constantly shock them to the core? Chasing ghosts and wanting to go back to some moments of the past, I force myself forward because that's the only way for me. Do I lie awake at night thinking about them? Yes. Do I want what every guy wants from them? Of course. I'll match it and raise you because as I toss and turn I can give them more than what they ever had. Yes, they have broken my heart and I can be heartbroken like everyone else but I repair it because gods and angels bleed, too. They also cry like everyone else but I'm going to be strong and fulfill this taboo if I have to. You can shove me away for it has been done, you can tie me and crucify me metaphorically, and you can take my soul. What hasn't been done to me? I can take it. I am prideful, wrathful, jealous and sometimes lost in my mind thinking about tomorrow. At other times I am patient, intelligent, resourceful, giving, forgiving, turn the other cheek and love more than the person next to me. My heightened emotions are a double edged sword I struggle with everyday as one day I can neglect them and make up for it the next moment. Will I learn from my mistakes? Yes. Will I learn to control my needs? Eventually. I will be everything I ever wanted to be and not apologize for who I am. One day, tomorrow, you will see my own Garden Of Eden and like it or not, it will be perfect enough for me all through my malicious yet beautiful kind ways. One day I will leave this earth and come back a few years later. Maybe.

No

No. Go. Stop. Come back. Leave. It's been a while. How have you been? Oh, me? Absolutely fantastic. No, my mind hasn't been scrambled. The soldiers on the ship? Gone. I've commandeered the ship. Weren't you supposed to protect me? What are you talking about? There's nothing but doubt. Racing thoughts on my mind. I've followed your orders blind. I've completed my mission and this is the price to pay? Can you show me the way? I make no sense because I don't know what is going on. The mind can go numb and crazy when you see the new dawn. Oh, hi, there. Where? There? Remember me? Did you leave before or after you threw my heart out to sea? Did you throw it on the ground and step on it, too? Or was it me that shot you with my blaster and hurt you? Oh, I'm sorry. I was the one that interrogated you and you sand like a canary. I was only doing what I thought was patriotic. Do you still have my unshattered mind saved in a hard drive that doesn't make me look psychotic? It seems like there is disastrous damage in my cerebral area. My immune system feels weak as if it were stricken by malaria. I have to keep myself composed and land to the nearest medical bay to heal myself completely. It's hard to stay sane when you sacrifice everything for the sake of the mission, the greater cause but maybe this death will come sweetly. Just delete me. I can go into deep sleep, hibernate and be unbothered. Reminiscent of the past I remember too well but wish to forget at times because it hurts too much and now I feel cornered. They say they regret leaving me and that's why they came back, they said I shot them in the back and twisted the knife, who to believe? A battered and scarred soldier too unstable and dangerous for anyone and now I need a new sleeve. This space odyssey is far from over but I still feel alone.

Daydream

I was laying down and remembering the day of a fire drill on a Friday. You left without your good jacket and put on a yellow sweater quickly. It was a little sweet gesture and I wrapped my blue jacket around you and it fit like a cape. I have nowhere to escape. You're on my mind mercilessly and endlessly and I'm trying to push it back. I treasure the moments I get to spend with you and the soundtracks remind me of you, makes me daydream about you and it gives me a little panic attack. I often wonder if I take no action will I really end up alone? I always feel that way but I want someone with me on my throne. It will be glorious having someone rule the galaxy with me reaching multiple milestones. I don't know what it is about you but you impress me. I'm pretty sure it is because you remind me of myself and you're a queen bee. You rule over your mini dominion elegantly. You dance with perfect rhythm and to the beat. I love how you are and you're so petite. When I joked around how my old jacket doesn't fit me, it fit you like a glove when I called you over as we all laughed about it and I felt complete. They said I deserve better, they said I deserve a woman that's a gem, will that be you or do I have to keep searching across the ocean and stars? Do I have to go above and beyond to find you on Mars? Daydreaming and thinking what it would be like when you invite me over while I bring the food. Talking, laughing and getting closer by the minute as you learn that I write poetry as my shyness rises to a higher altitude. I'm not screwed because I can shake it off with my abundant confidence, read an excerpt and catch you smiling really hard with your teeth showing and your cheeks flushed bright red. You ask me if it's about you as I take a sip of my drink and nod my head slowly, smirking and saying, "who else would it be?" You'll tell me how the words made you feel and how it was good. We'll spend an evening together as my cologne will be a constant reminder of me even when I'm gone. Walking me to the door, you'll ask me what I'm thinking about right now as I stare into your eyes and lips that turn me on. I hold your waist and tummy and ask you if I'll get in trouble for kissing you. You smile again without saying anything but doing nothing to prevent it. I lean slowly and nervously towards you and you meet me halfway and like a puzzle, we perfectly fit. You lift your leg up like they do in the movies of the 50s and tell me to get home safely, to text you when I arrive home. Right as I get in the car to be driven home, a booming gunshot sound of thunder wakes me up from a daydream that makes it sour like the attitude of a gnome. I lay back down and remember the fond memories to feel good on the inside. Patiently having to maintain my bipolar nature of impatience and lord knows I tried. Just a little bit longer until I finally see you while we are trapped. I'll keep daydreaming of you because it's the only therapy I know of that will help me adapt.

I Remember Why

It's been all the same but I have had my eyes shut for so long. This pain, this anger, this hatred, the overwhelming sadness with my hypersensitivity I blocked away all along. Thirteen years later and it's still the same! I have no shame. There is nothing to acclaim my name. The same story where my unrequited love gets the best of me, my poor decisions and acting on impulse that gets me stuck time and time again. I am so tired of hearing people say I deserve better. I am tired of hearing people say I will find someone one day but how long will that take now that I am older and stronger? I remember someone said what is the point of traveling alone and what will I do all alone in my hotel room, that traveling with a partner will make the trip exponentially more memorable. How can I if nobody seems to care about me romantically? How can I when nobody shows me that they can love me? How can I when every time I try I get rejected so much that it gets discouraging to try again even after I recover? Tell me! Believe me when I say I really am trying my hardest to not intentionally look for love because it will find me but how does it feel when I somehow repel people away from me? How does it feel when I finally fall for someone and their actions seem to be true at first, they slither away? How long do I have to fake a smile when the inner parts of me that are fighting away the negativity will make me turn away from your deities, all that is good, all that is human when I constantly find myself having bad things happen to me? I fight through the pool of it, I swim in it, I am drowning in it and find my way back to the light. Every time I wipe away the tears because I am truly scared of what I can become and the light in me dims down, losing how bright it can be. I deserve all of this, perhaps, maybe I don't. I am not sure what to make of this when people are close to me and slowly walk away and I won't have any of it! I cannot handle this anymore but I know I can take the beating. The senseless pain of loss, losing something I never had with an isolation so deep it runs cold in my veins. Chronic loneliness, unreciprocated, disillusioned, all of these I have lived my entire life and I have made myself stronger for it but at the cost of a damaged mind. I may have finally resigned. I remember my old ways, the volcanic bouts of anger, the tornadoes of sadness, the earth quaking hatred that I have to hide away and keep it together. I just don't care anymore and if I have to I will revert back to my old ways because I am a survivor. You all will never hear from me again. Prove me wrong or get out of the way because I have nothing left to gain. I am trying everyday to pull myself from my laces but the constant fragmentation of my foundations is being tested time and time again and you seem to pass when the horns grow out, my wings burn and my tail grows. Do you want to see what I can do? Fine! I will show you! I understand why some of the other gods dislike the mortals so much. In a blink of an eye you will see the 180 as you feel my touch. It will burn you inside out. Hype me up to bring me down again is your last mistake and I won't sit here and pout. I will bring myself to do it and leave before I hurt anyone I still love. People say I am not missing much but what they don't understand is that the missing piece of having a hole in my heart, a lack of love I have not felt and don't know what it's like, the constant worry of starting over with people who don't seem to care about me, I get it, and I will keep putting myself above all. I will rip out my own throat before I feel another heavy hurt in my own heart, the pounding in my chest, the knot in my throat and my eyes go watery as people only care about me and butter me up when they want something from me. No more. I will keep my distance and turn my heart of gold to rust and steel. Everyone will be kept at an arm's length for a while. You won't know what I'm thinking and my aggressive nature will keep me hostile. It was all of you that triggered my actions, my stupid feelings and the reproach I have known all along. Destroying me is your own downfall. I can feel the aura from me turning from white to black and I fade away in the darkness.

Still

It's been some time since I've destroyed the planet I have loved for so long. I have no sense of where I belong. I am still greedy and I wonder why I still care. I went to the far away galaxies and destroyed the other civilizations and it isn't fair. I went to other timelines and destroyed everything again repeatedly, unforgivingly and aimlessly. I threw a giant tantrum because things didn't go my way and I still feel the same as I have done years ago without a plea. I was supposed to help these people and apparently I was the chosen one but I joined a darker side. I am still hungry for love but it looks like I haven't reached that point of redemption, sucking the life force of people, eating everything away and letting things wither and die. I have ripped apart planes, cities, people, and governments to show them my pain all in vain. Many have stood up to me but they were no match because they didn't train. They were weak naturally and even when they worked as one it wasn't enough to put a strain. The only thing that can hurt me is myself with my memories and my sensitivity. Many will call me crazy, over reactive and blind to my own blessings but I see no end to this, no light as of right now, and I have crumbled into pieces long ago. I did try but I was being cut into pieces and although I am in agony, my pride will not let it go. I will surpass this no matter what it is I have to do. I look at how before people had love from others even when they were bad and did everything to sabotage it. I always wondered how some people were loved like that and I hated it because nobody loved me like that. Sure, I have been, but the love of a family is drastically different from the love of a woman. You're not going to cuddle with your mother, make love to your brother, and bring roses to your father, are you? Absolutely not. As I sit here on the ledge of a mountain with the world slowly burning in flames, the skies black, a lightning storm that encompasses my feelings, I try to think where it all went wrong. I remember those positive books that keep reminding people that we are all worthy of love and if I'm so great, if my personality is unlike another other, if I really was pure and handsome, then why haven't I gotten it yet? Where are these so-called affections that exist or do I have to forget about it? I offer it so many times for them to spit it back at my face. I wipe it off and burn myself and force a genuine smile and no matter how I turn the glass to get a different perspective of happiness, seeing a new light, there is nothing to chase or replace. You've all let a loser and inferior level of people break your heart but I let just about anyone wipe the floor with me and leave a dirty, iron taste of filth in my mouth.

Drink my Soul

After this whole prison life is over, I will pay my dues and drink the wine in. I will visit the unforgivable of vices and drown in them. I will be dazed and busy that will help me not think about it all. The willpower I had to face the music is done and I will have to live for myself during this fall. I won't even glance back and buy love if I have to. If I can't get it naturally and people are unwilling to be vulnerable with me, uncaring of me and keeping me around for their amusement then I will have to turn myself into a basket case, too. With all the money I have will be spent to feel the affections of a woman, have that delicate touch and make them fake the words that I will have to pretend I love to hear. I will force myself to have butterflies in my stomach like I did when I was younger. I will forget them all and push it aside and spend time with the exotic dancer. I cry tears of sadness as she dances on me, sings to me and caresses my face, wiping the tears. They'll ask me what's wrong but I just skip them a bill to make me feel better. I won't be sober for much longer these days as my feelings lessen but it's whatever. Drink with me or don't, I wonder how many of you know what it's truly like. Or maybe you won't. Maybe I'm too superficial and silly to see what's in front.

Stop

That's enough, I won't continue with this weakness. Time to stop feeling sorry for myself in a time of distress. I have to pick myself up, bring myself up because there is no one who will love me more than I give the love I give myself. I don't care anymore because I won't be a shell of what I once was or leave my soul on a shelf. My name is John and so far I haven't seen a person worth my time. I will stand up for myself, believe in myself and bring my own self worth and it won't matter if nobody believes in me. I don't care if I will stay alone because I will inspire everything and everyone to the point where I will have everyone under my shade like a tree. If you used me, abused me, mistreated me, took me for granted you will regret it when I leave because my time is now. You will recognize my worth, you will know better and you will bow. My soul can be tainted and damaged but I will give myself the strength not even Superman can do himself because he needs the sun. I have no sun, I have no one special, I have no second half and no soul mate other than myself because I am worth a ton. I'll slap myself silly for being this week again. There is a reason I left the old me behind and won't turn against the grain. Hype me up? I will do just that. Betray me? You go first before I won't make the time of day for that and even when you do I'll brush myself off. Stick two middle fingers to you at your face, close up like HD for making me feel as if I wasn't worth anything and feel bad about myself. Put this missing sense of affection I put so much tears on and you can shove it up where the sun doesn't shine and leave me by myself. You can make fun of me all you want but I went back and forth in time to right the wrongs I made. Time to stop acting like a baby and a fool, I'll be someone you'll drool over.

Unreceptive

Catching feelings for someone you spend quite a long time with is something that happens naturally. Then you get embarrassed because their actions show they don't feel the same and it gets confusing when they did, truly. Sometimes I feel stupid as I did fearlessI feel the sadness of Peter

Parker when his uncle died, the pain of extreme loss and discomfort of Barry Allen when his mother was murdered, the unending mental torture when Bruce Wayne lost his parents in the alleyway. Suffering in silence always. I am destroyed by pain and hold the weight of the world in my shoulders. The constant embarrassment of unrequited devotions and affections makes me feel stupid. I back down and lock myself away to bother and annoy you feeling wounded. I look at Cupid and ask him why his arrows hit the hearts of people that want nothing to do with me? Exaggerating the constant mishaps makes great for a dramatic novel as it chips away some of my happiness, my soul and gives me heartbreak. I always make people feel better but when I try to make myself feel better, it works only for a short time and as the night hits I feel the emotions that make my head and heart ache. It's all my fault because I got my hopes a little bit, just for one little heart warming message and I begin to wonder why. Sometimes I don't talk to others for long periods of time and get surprised when someone talks to me, do they really remember and think about me? How do you remember I exist? Who told you about me? I reflect and see how according to naysayers, people want to be loved without loving others. Am I the same? I don't know for sure. They say there is very little needed to be happy but how do I really know that whenever I try to reach out it gets shut down quickly? Overthinking this might be the death of me but I can't help how I feel and I have to move on quickly. The little feelings of constant rejection plays tricks on my mind rapidly. It's hard to control when that's all I have ever known.

Bad Boy

After some months in quarantine with my hair long, curly and wavy, almost disheveled but not really, I see you after a long, long time. With my shades on, I see you from a distance as I play along nonchalantly but my heart beats so fast it is going double time as my temperature begins to climb. It's summertime and it's hot but you're just so cool. You can't hide your excitement either as we power walk to each other as you throw your arms towards me, hugging me as I hold you down by your waist, lingering, resting our heads on each other's developed shoulders as all the problems in the world become minuscule. After a long, brief moment, my hands are still cusping your waist as I stare into your eyes but you can't see mine, smiling and asking me if I missed you. "What do you think? Of course I missed you. Every damn day. I used up some 11:11 wishes for this moment." You lead me into the classroom to talk about the lesson plans for the day. I take off my shades and I stare at you, eyes swimming all over your body and you suppress a smile and pretend it didn't happen anyway. Your pink polo shirt with your jean shorts that shows off the best features of your waist and legs, along with dirty converses that's white with a red lining around the sole. I slowly walk towards you and lean in for another hug, telling how much I needed you and I let go. We're standing way too close as I slowly fix your hair, tucking it behind your ear as I tell you how it bothered me and it needed to perfectly flow. I slowly massage your head but you don't put up a fight, enjoying the gentle strokes like a cat. With my free hand pushing you towards the table, making you sit. Now I place my hands slowly on your thighs and give you a gentle squeeze and you give a little gasp. Then I press on harder, leaving my hand prints on them as I hold your face on my hand, staring at each other's lips. I look at them longingly and you give a little giggle, then I push myself gently closer on you and move on slowly to place my lips gently on yours. One after another, I can feel the nervousness go away as you pull some of my hair. Gasping for breath, you start cheesing at me and I place my thumb on your lips, saying we can sneak a few more before the kids come. "I'm a bad boy with good intentions.", I whisper to her ear and we both feel a big dumb. It's hard to move when we are both frozen but I go in for another kiss as I give her waist a gentle squeeze as she lays her arms around my neck. This is perfect, a good start to the summer of 2020. My hands creep lower and lift her leg and wrap it around me, holding the delicious thickness of it as she laughs and punches my arm. I move back, pretending like nothing happened but give her a devilish smirk and wink at her, preparing for what would have been another innocent day at work.

Easy?

6 years ago a counselor asked what I wanted to be when I sought help. I wanted to make money to help out my parents and said I would just be a teacher, something remotely easy because it's what I felt. I needed the money, I felt stuck, I needed a way out and I wasn't going to sell myself out to the lowest bidder. I had a plan but I needed money for it, to be

something better and bigger. She said what am I going to tell them in the interview? I want to be a teacher because it's easy? Really? Would you think I'd be that stupid to have that as a response? Were you me that day or did you just place me in a box? You don't understand because you thought I was an idiot but I'm smarter than I look. Any job I could have grabbed my hands on would set me free but no matter how many ways I put it for you, explained it in different ways, it didn't get through your thick skull, huh? Look at me now and analyze because what I have to say is an earful. I've made my money work for me while I thrift. Don't get me upset because you'll see how much I lift. I sought out the help from myself because that was the only way, I guess. At 23 I found a way out temporarily and struggled through and through like everyone else. Long hours staring at boxes all day while I got annoyed at the impatient call outs. The best sound is hearing the radio turn off after 8 hours to head straight home, tired, for long showers. Anger, frustration, short tempers kept me from being stepped on as barking orders left and right as I tried to keep my mouth shut until I let it roam free, a mind of its own. From a little scared cat to a savage tiger in the forest I spoke to them in a different tone. I growled my way up and I was ready for a fight as badly as I instigated it. Tempted to slap people silly but trying to keep my composure because it wasn't worth it. Fast forward to another tough year I got the taste of power. A few hours here and there and I saw how the other half lived. I got addicted to it and through my way I found an upgraded version of me, at least financially. Pop the champagne because it's been a long road and living life on automatic, I don't even have to count how many checks I have to work to get what I want and it feels fantastic. Don't test me because the problem will go away faster than water running through your fingers. Hype myself up because I'm back on it and for the longest time I finally feel like a winner. It doesn't matter how cocky I was before, it's nothing like you'll ever see because my mind goes faster than a gun slinger. New ideas popping up, racing words that make me stutter, I am a complex thinker. Shoot them with facts, hurt them with my words, push them into a corner with my experience and teach them I can torture them mentally if they crawl under my skin. Revelations say to keep yourself humble but so far I've had dirty looks and mumbles. Testing me is all you can do and I will pass every time and shock you, don't do it, you'll crumble. So now, Miss Counselor, I'll tell you all I ever wanted was experience to get a job to set my talented self to shoot for the stars and become one but I guess you didn't really know how to express the answers, did you? I do get that nothing comes easy but a little push to guide me to my destiny was all I needed earlier but I had to do that on my own. Look at me now, it's toxic I know, but you'll see the success that maybe your own children will have trouble finding. It's not about the Midas touch but it's about having the brains and belief that you will do it. It's the mental toughness and the invaluable charisma to launch myself upwards, higher than the clouds.

Vampiric Energy

Seeing you all drenched from water in your sports bra outfit makes me lose it. Swimsuit model, all lean with defined features from your cheekbones to her shapely legs and thin shoulders. It will feel warm in between your legs and the sensations will be in the eyes of the beholder. You pull my thick hair back and massage my head at the same time. You're aesthetically pleasing to look at and keeping this to myself would be a crime. You don't need any makeup or voluptuous body parts because you're all natural. Gently sitting on your tooshy and giving you a foundation of several kisses on your back will be multilateral. I want to feel the fabric of your clothes as you bite down my neck, dripping water from the spandex as you move closer, our bodies touching as you give me a small peck. I can feel it, it's soft as your hair falls on my arm as my heart is racing, feeling a good count, pulse on check. Not saying this just to flatter you because these are all facts. Being hunters of the night, during the dark time is when we best shine and in this we made a small pact. To stimulate your mind and excite your dopamines is all I want. Luxurious French lips that are fuller than life that I want to feel on my skin that feels so much more refined and delicious than food from a five star restaurant. I'll bathe in you and feel the taste of champagne surrounded in water of bubble baths, warm enough to tickle. I want you to model just for me as I have for you, being your personal swimsuit model for the years to come. Maybe it'll make you shy but I want to bring the animal out of you that's inside, a wild one that won't get off me like bubblegum. I want to spend several nights with you and release the passions as if I'll be gone tomorrow, as if it'll be my last.

You can be small and delicate but be rough and tough with me while I'm big and strong like a bear so I can be able to lift you up, feel my strength so you can feel protected and make your head spin with excitement and determination.

My body is my gift to you, I want you to own me, possess me and do what you want to do with me like it's Christmas. You're the tigress that can tame this beast. When I'm with you it feels like summer, to say the least. All the vibrant colors of the flowers you can see, you can taste the freshness in the air and feel the heat of the sun at the peak of its finest hour. You want attention? I'm eager to please. You want pleasure? I'm sweeter than candy and your taste buds will agree. I'll make you erupt like a volcano and we'll be exhausted as if we had driven in the Grand Prix. I'll lose sleep just thinking about you. I'll be stuck in your mind so much that you'll dream of me, replacing the constant nightmares. Your laughter will be engraved in my mind.

This time around I'll remove your self doubts and kiss away the traumas to your fullest satisfaction. Drink all the blood you want, feed from me and live on. I'll come back for more because I'm a glutton for punishment and I can take it.

Dark Knight

Come in like Batman at night and message you before my arrival. I climb into your bedroom from the window preparing for something vital. Giggling quietly we close the door so we can have fun on the bed sheets but not too loud before they hear us. It's just me and you and that's a huge plus. Having to muffle our sounds and screams, it's exciting almost getting caught, knowing the risk. You play around with my hair as I give you a meaningful frisk. Let's put it to the test and see who wins at giving the other the most pleasure. I'll be Peter Parker and you Mary Jane since you're a redhead, after all, and I'll make sure to meet your demands, standards,your fantasies all beyond measure. I'll tangle you up and explore different positions with you. We can have fun all night long and I can sneak away before anyone wakes up and I will make you say "ooh!". You can kiss me softly and surprise me more with your kinks. It'll be hard resisting moaning your name loudly so I'll have to settle for gentle whispers as I bite tenderly at your ear. I want to feel the taste of you everyday and never get tired of it and everything I want to hear. I'll make love to you every single day. It'll be blasphemy under the jealous angels because you're going to be all mine as I am all yours and maybe they'll make me pay. I want to trace along my gentle fingers across your juicy legs as you tremble with excitement, biting your lips in the process. Your giggle just gives me an extra boost to kiss down your chest, your stomach, your waist, and even licking your piercings in curious parts. We can sneak in various love making sessions between the sheets more passionate than ever because nobody is going to stop us. You can cusp your hands on my face and tell me how beautiful I am, as I stare into your lustful green eyes and admire the bright and vivid color of it. You can make this heart of steel go away, you can pierce through my icicle armor as I tear down your walls. We can repeat the magic over and over and want more of each other. We are each other's fallen angels and we make each other's day exponentially better. I'll hold your head softly and make you kiss my chest, my shoulders, my muscular arms and even my legs. I won't hold back as I grab you by the ankles and spoil you with kisses across your thighs, bite down your calves, and lick almost in between your thighs with a passion that burns hotter than fire. You'll enjoy the love bites, gentle squeezes that'll make you scream as I muffle your voice down with my hand covering your mouth. I'll enjoy playing, touching and kissing your juicy legs and going down south. You'll hold my head down as I finally fulfill your hungry needs and beautiful sensational kisses across your body as I make you mine. You'll never want this to end as the minutes feel like days with each pressing and pushing moment. You'll bite your lips so much just waiting for it to finish to yet start again, adoring the anticipation that makes everything so much better. You recently said not to trust your photos because you're not that pretty in real life, but how is it every time I see even a little smile from you I am set on fire? All I have to do is look at you and I'm sailing across the ocean. So bring that fine and sexy self over here and bust it open because I'll give you everything with strong emotion. I'll treat you right, spoil you endlessly and you will see that it's true because you're the one I want to give it to.

Preoccupied and Busy

Addicted to the gambling life only because I've been winning and winning. All I see is green and no hearts even though I want it so badly. It's 11:11 and instead of wishing for you I just wish for a million more wishes because I'm not sure if you're down for me truly. I can't blame you for being busy but it still is a bit discouraging to not hear back from you. Now I'm just vibing by myself and I don't want to disappoint you, too. It's supposed to come naturally but what if I all for another yet again because you distanced yourself from me and I've done the same. Will you hate me forever if you tell me you actually liked me but I'm with someone else? I can't help but wonder about my unknown future but at this point in time it's like a pendulum swing and it's quite complex. It's not that I can't make up my mind but when they show a lack of interest, or at least how I perceive it to be, I tend to fall back and move on to make progress. I actually do miss you but after all of what I've tried, I can't force it or beg you so I'll just take a wild guess. The small affections I seem to cling to, whomever that is generous to show it to me and how beautifully it is expressed. Keeping my head on straight, I only see tomorrow. I have to go forward and keep loving on despite my sorrow. I am tangled and intertwined with what I thought I knew yesterday, what I know now, and how the table will turn tomorrow that'll betray me yet again. I thought I found my golden ticket but that's okay, I still have a chance to recover it and claim my prize. She said we can kiss underwater and I highly look forward to that. I wish it'll come to a manifestation. I'm working hard through this realization. I just honestly don't know and by the time we get back, I'll be asked about you but what can I say? I tried and it didn't work and that's okay. It's not a race but I wonder who will actually steal my heart today and keep me forever way past until my last day.

Crazy

It's hard battling emotions that constantly betray a rational mind. I'm finding my way out of this tunnel and see the light at the end of it but I'm still blind. I am blinded by the darkness when I do reach the end. It's a perfect blend. Trying to not lash out and explode and a daily battle to not let them get ahold of it. It's difficult when one is constantly ignored and unsettled when they find peace in solitude. Trying my best not to catch feelings because they'll betray me at the end of the day and it's always in this magnitude. I'm trying my best not to feed into it and to leave people alone for a while. It doesn't matter how much I explain myself, the words won't make it any better and even I get annoyed at the little things but I have to hide it with a smile. Gritting my teeth against each other until my gums bleed only to wipe it off my lips because this aspect of being over sensitive kills me slowly. There's a threshold I'm learning to increase because I have to make myself stronger exponentially. I'm tired of it sometimes, I just rather avoid the situation and even get angry when my thoughts are constantly interrupted time and time again, sucking my teeth in the process. It makes my head hurt and it's difficult to suppress. I'm trying to go on about my day as usual but then I get reminded and even when I tell myself I'm fine I come across as someone who solely cares about success. I can't even function properly and takes a whole day of torture just to feel fine again. Controlling my emotions is a constant strain and quite difficult to maintain. I'm trying to disappear and shut it down because it doesn't make sense to stress out over something mundane. I can tell myself all this but no matter what, it's still in my brain. I'm trying to cut off the speed of my thoughts as I'm praying to not deal with dry conversations I get annoyed at. What comes after nine? Ten, and that's how many times I broke my spine. I'm shape shifting into something I'm trying not to become because it's hateful to act like a child as an adult. I can't look back and need a consult to find my end result. My body is cold and cannot fight the infections, the windy breezes don't help and now I'm ready to be taken. I've survived this long and now I'd like you to lay my body to rest and maybe I'm mistaken, but wake me up when it's 2040. I need to rest in the cryogenic chamber. You don't have to remember me, I just need some rest and a fresh start for the remainder of my long life.

Vibing

You're worth being on time for and I remember the day I came in late, as they told me you made a little disappointed frown as they asked about me. Remembering small details about you just to make myself sane again and when I first heard about that I was dancing in my mind gleefully. Everything is going fast, you can be the Iris West to my Barry Allen. I'm running at superspeed trying to delete my memory but the red streak follows suit and the feelings are filling up faster by the gallon. Your smile makes my day and I love the warm, fuzzy feeling I felt but that might just be in the past. I'm a hopeless romantic in a hookup culture, nobody believes in love anymore but I want something that lasts. I'm waiting to run into someone to give them all of my heart and soul with a blast. I've been used and led on that I can't tell the difference anymore. You're smile worthy but maybe I've crashed into a locked door. I can run faster than the speed of light, take a light jog at the speed of sound, but I'm nowhere near you. Time is something I may have but it's gone faster than the sand slipping through my fingers. The same slippage of water that passes through my body and I'm trying to make sense of all this. I'm just vibing away and easing my mind of mental constellations and destruction, adjusting one detail in the nick of time. All I can do is run because I'm faster than The Flash but I'm still a wreck because I've used up all my rhymes. Shuffling my feet in sync with the beats and drums, I'm fighting and dancing away moments of weakness. It doesn't matter how many lives I save, I'm no doctor. It doesn't matter how many points in time I travel to, I just want to see you dancing along and kissing me in alternate timelines. You've made me weak, it's not bleak, it's more human than ever and your soul to contaminate mine is all I seek. I need your energy, but not to drain you, but I need the same positive vibes I felt a few months ago. I lived in a bubble but I still see your face, I still cherish your smile and I'm trying to fight against it and I just don't know. I wear a symbol on my chest but maybe the lightning in my heart that beats for you will hurt me in the end. The sooner I realize it, the sooner I can fade away into the future with no memory yet the time remnants makes me continue this crush on you. Maybe I'm just insane and have seen and been in too many things in my life I wouldn't believe.

Downhearted

It's hard to not take things personally, but lately it's hard to control the blues. How can I not when I haven't heard from you over a week, how can I choose? It would be nice to be checked up on by you but I guess I'm a little crazy. It doesn't matter because I'm a little luney. I'm trying to get a hold of myself but I'm like Tony Stark, a millionaire with everything from the tip of his finger yet I feel like I still have nothing. I'm worried over little things that don't matter and all I can do is keep running. It's annoying when they say I do weird things like catch feelings and don't want me to like them, but how can I when we talk daily and spend so much time with each other? I get attached quite easily. How can that be said and avoided when we are around each other frequently? Your skin is the warmest color. I want to hold you and kiss you along the traces of your neck but I'm yanked off by reality, trying to psychoanalyze me and continue to suffer. I'm still worried the affections are shown to me because of quarantine and when it's over, will I see you again for real? Sometimes I can be crazy and cheerful on the outside while other times I'm dark and brooding, quiet for most of the time, pretending it's not a big deal. Different people get different versions of me because they all bring that out in me, showing what I feel. I can be indifferent and nonchalant if I don't care but if I find the appeal, different parts of my character shows. My heart has gone cold along with my body, my soul is shrouded in icy mists. Keeping my head up high with eyes looking down, clenching my fists. Maybe there's a hole in my heart and the internal struggle between happiness and anger collide, a love child that is sadness. Why am I sad? I can't find enough legitimate reasons and that's bad. Melodramatic is my middle name, you don't want this life. You don't want to know what's really going on inside my head, it's an everlasting strife. The conflict is that I know I shouldn't be looking for anything externally when I am complete internally, yet my inner peace is disrupted when people come and go in my life, distracting me from my goals. Crossing my path just to make me feel things I know I shouldn't and the disappointment you feel when you asked for little gifts for Christmas but instead you open up boxes containing coals. They say the most dangerous animal in the zoo is your reflection, all I see is a broken lion mending his wounds. I have no idea why these patterns exist, there must be something missing from my childhood. I'm a bad thing, everything I touch withers away and dies, or maybe it's the bad things that wither and die, transferring it all to me. Maybe. Draining the negativity and absorbing it, reasonable explanation? I don't know but it makes sense, this strange combination. My addictions are catching up with me, that's not good medication. It's easy to block out your emotions when your heart is made of stone. My heart is made from glass and reflects my perception of the world, many things shown. My sins are catching up with my, the karma I'm paying for day in and day out. I don't like how this is turning out, I'm not right in the head and I need to shout.

Cybernetic Soul

I'm at the beach at night, feeling the droplets of water forming from the rain. The gusts of wind try to push me back as I remember the sweet dame. I feel the vibrations of gravity, pushing and pulling the ocean in waves. I trace it through with my hands, my arms, waning and waxing like the moon as the water fills in the caves. I am dancing like a water bender. If I die tomorrow, I want to visit my own funeral, maybe dying from an important mission, maybe from a tragic accident or an unforeseen disease. I'd see how my funeral plays out,witness who will shed a tear for the body in the coffin in the six foot grave. I want to see the reactions, the emotional wrecks, the collapses, I want to witness who feels my absence to what extremity. Maybe I'd get amnesia from hitting my hard way too hard, I would be called a liar but I just don't know you but I can feel the chemistry. Disappearing and being invisible like water vapor, you'll never see me again. Liar. Will you really cry for me or be happy I'm gone? Perhaps I was recruited and brainwashed to serve my country the best way possible in the form black ops, mutating my genes. Too many battles, too many scars, you would not recognize me as everything within me changed to every cell to each detail of my proteins. We would walk past each other one day and you would do double take at me, a small glimpse of someone you remember but you are sure it isn't me because I died long ago. It couldn't be me, can it? The same facial structure, same youthful look with sad eyes with scars across my eye slit. The color of my hair changed to bright silver, it makes you shiver. You are much older now, never the same and apparently me being gone has affected you much more than anticipated. Maybe it is just as expected. Gone without my love and too late to do anything about it, you'll never know how great it would have been if I took care of you, spoiled you, and woke up next to each other without a care in the world. I wouldn't recognize you but you pull me back anyway because you had to, you couldn't resist it. I look at you with a hateful scorn, eyes bluer than crystalline meth. I promised you I would stay forever, no matter what, and how my bond will never break, even beyond death. You rattle me as you can't help but see the person I used to be. I shove you onto the ground believing you're a crazy person I never met and continue to my destination. You make a fool of yourself, grabbing onto my leg and never letting go as I get angry, tossing you a platinum coin as if you required a donation. You noticed my cold, metallic black arm ready to engage into combat mode. You shed a tear, then you slowly cry in a river. "Where is the sweet boy who didn't let the world change him? Where is the compassion and love he felt for people, even those that he hated? Where was the one of a kind person who was bright that made me feel better just talking to him? What happened to you?" Annoyed at what I was hearing, I had no idea what this strange woman was talking about, tempted to end her misery but not in front of the eyes of an entire city. "40 years gone into the future and even though you changed, how can you still look the same?" You beg and plead for answers I do not have. Liar. Still, even though my memory has been wiped clean I still shed a tear.. Liar. I don't know this woman yet I feel something vaguely familiar. She takes out her phone and shows me the time I have missed, photos of my family I lost. Liar. I don't know these people and I told her my soul has been laid to rest, affectionate or not I became frost. I am not the person you are looking for and whomever he may be, he is forever lost. You let every ounce of failed relationships make you cold and bitter then and when you had this person in your vicinity, you cherished him but it was still too late. "And after all this time, now you say you want me back? You want the old me again? I don't know what to tell you, old woman. I am not who you say I am and even if I was, I am pretty sure I wouldn't ever come back." Liar. I turn away from her and set my boosters to fly off wondering who she might be. A few miles in the distance I look back just one time to see her still weeping on the concrete floor.

Cyberpunk

When I was recruited by the military, I thought I only signed a 4 year contract. I did it to get away from you, doing my best to avoid you at all costs to save myself from the embarrassment because you gave my heart such a shocking impact. I only did it with the intention of coming back to you, testing out to see if you'd truly reach out to me because I miss you. A cowardly move that I soon will pay the price and I will be distant from myself, too. After filling out my psych evaluation and passing the physical exams with flying colors, they took me to a clinic. It was supposed to be part of a super soldier program but with one injection I saw the horror that became prolific. I could feel it eating at me on the inside, the pain and felt the change in my DNA. It was a series of horrible transformations and hallucinations. These allegations were true. Next thing I knew I had eerie blue eyes and my hair turned silver. They somehow managed to delete my memories from the past, locked it away and I wouldn't get to see it because it all became unfamiliar. It started out with testing my abilities so they can see what I can do. Part of a death squad, I succeeded in every suicide mission they sent me, in the middle of a zoo. In the middle of no safety and bullets swooshing everywhere. My animalistic instincts kicked in and I unleashed an unholy fury. I became a force of evil to be feared. I only knew how to engage in this senseless violence, sharpening my skills for the highest bidder and eager to get the job done with the blood of my enemies smeared. I zone out in the moment as the years go on by, never aging, never growing, never truly thinking. Everything was natural to me, it was scary, not making any mistakes as I became numb to everything. Taking lives as easily as stepping on roaches, the weapons evolving from bullets to pulses and energy-like bullets, the sun being weaponized. Lasers, overpowered artillery that will do more than injury. The scars became more apparent through my reckless behavior. Someone tried to slit my throat but I parried it away as they sliced my face, which would heal just fine but barely enough as the energy blade cut some pieces of my skin on my left eye. I tossed my head back in time and flinched but the sight of dripping blood from my brow made me lose it. I dropped my gun and began head hunting, blow after blow, bruising my enemy to the point they couldn't even be saved by a first aid kit. I picked up his energy blade as a souvenir. Left hand with the rifle, right hand with the blade as I took down the numbers left and right, even if they had the perfect gear. A million miles away from home and no one can save me from myself. A few years after that I took my favorite blade for another mission, some good hunting, but it was no match for the upgraded anti tank rifles that tore off my right arm clean. Wounded but not finished, I unleash my rage from forgotten memories where the unloved, misguided, unwanted and wrongly placed faith where my redemption would be unseen. I know I am not fooling anyone and I barely made it, bringing hellfire on everything around me in a 10 square foot mile radius. All of this just for delaying a political proposal that would benefit the elites. The chopper took me to the nearest medical bay where I was given some care, a gift, a cybernetic right arm to punish the freedom fighters and criminals in the eyes of the United Government. Looking in the mirror, I see how much I have changed on the inside as much as I have on the outside and my mental state is fried. Am I really living? All I hear is the noise in a quiet room. As they operate on me, a tear falls out not from the excruciating physical pain but from what I became. Cursing everyone I come across because everyone and everything I ever loved was taken from me. What have they done to me? Am I really their best creation? Mirror mirror on the wall, am I really the nastiest of them all? I suffer from temporary thunderclap headaches that make me see glimpses of a past I do not recall ever living in. I took a walk in the city to cancel out the noise in my head and a silly old lady wouldn't let me go. We came across each other and she acted quite strangely until I pushed her away, not remembering nor caring who she was. I left her sobbing on the ground as I flew away and that's when it hit me. I'm crying because the chemistry was familiar, her scent, her voice but I couldn't quite place it and I had to have a word with my maker. I need to make this right and see about this faker. Was this the woman I loved before and tried to escape or was she another heartbreaker?

I Hope I Get To See You In September

Wishing and wishing, missing you and missing you, not a day goes by that I don't think about your beautiful yet funny oval shaped head. I laugh to myself for roasting you in my mind, but in the end I guess I still like you. I'm strange because I also like other people at the same time, probably makes me a hypocrite to everything I stand for, too. The spring is halfway done and we're stuck and I'm running out of luck. Toss a coin in the fountain and see if I can get a bigger bang for my buck. I tested out one wish and I closed my eyes. When I opened them, I found myself a few months ahead where everything is finally done and the virus finally dies. My hair is longer yet the sides and back faded beautifully. My top hair falls down in a curtain style where my bangs fall across my face asymmetrically. My body is toned again yet leaner, as the old days when I used to weight train. Looking through the reflection from a car window, I have some stylish aviators with my hair tousled, short sleeve light denim dress shirt, khaki joggers and some Forrest Gump Cortez's. "Damn, you look fine.", someone says. I turned around but I couldn't tell who said that.

I walk the familiar path to the school, hands in my pockets, the moment I dreamed of finally coming back. Greeting cheerfully and hugging companions left and right, I see you from a short distance. It urged me and I couldn't hold down the resistance. A few inches away and you finally turn to me saying how you missed me so very much as you threw yourself at me, hugging me unusually harder than you normally do. I'm shocked that you even said that and are doing this, but I slowly put my arms around your narrow waist and hug you back, squeezing you, never wanting to let go and we're stuck like glue. "There hasn't been a single day I haven't thought about you. You're a sight for sore eyes." You giggle nervously and instinctively feel my hair as my hands are still holding you by the waist but you don't seem to mind but I wonder if this is unwise. "Your hair grew. I like it. You've also gotten...bigger." As she unsubtly feels my arm and lays her hand to feel my chest, she's a heavy hitter. I had nothing to say so I just removed my aviators to gaze at your eyes dreamily. Your eyes twinkle as you unconsciously grin at me. We can't seem to let go of each other as people pass by us, grinning at a real life soap opera and sitcom, their favorite couple that they've shipped since I was the new boy from the block. We snapped out of it as I nervously looked down like a little shy boy but you raised my chin, grabbed me by the hand and locked the door behind us and you aim at my lips like a hawk. You lose control of yourself and prowl on me like a cougar. You push me to your little roller chair and sit on my lap, raging hormones taking over and living out a final fantasy and this is my future. We lose ourselves in each other, hands all over without bounds but we hear the bell ring. You get off me and fix yourself, pretending nothing happened but you gave me the special, seductive, Scorpio look I've been wanting since the spring.

Nice and Easy

It's been some time throughout this whole wave of misery but you always said I make your day better. It always makes me grin like an idiot as if I got a notice in the mail, saying I won the lottery in a letter. I always appreciated how you are on the inside as well as your looks and that always catches you off guard because you just don't see it. Living in a shadow for so long you doubt yourself but I always see the beauty in you and I love everything about you, every little bit. I'll kiss every part of your scars and listen to everything you can't say to a trusted medic because I've inspired trust between us. We have this cherished bond that always takes long to discuss. Those lovely green eyes that only a small percentage of people have, your silky hair that smells like coconuts and sugar mixed with apples. I always stutter mentally when you come across my mind and always joke with you, especially laughing at your giant Snapple. Nobody ever wrote you poems until I came along. Nobody does it like me and it never feels wrong. You somehow eat up the words that make you melt and heavily appreciate. Despite everything that happened in your life, I still make you feel safe and you turn bright red at times, your cheeks flushing, when I say sweet things that's going quite well at this rate. You're several miles away but that doesn't stop me from seeing you, riding in the back of a Lexus, phoning you, anticipating the excitement. I don't know how but we both have a powerful attachment. Even though you've gone cold through the years, my little gestures make you question yourself. Finally climbing out the car with a rose in my hand, you playfully roll your eyes saying that flowers die but mine is made of intrinsic plastic that never dies. You laugh at the ingenuity. We go for lunch and enjoy the summer breeze. Every now and then we both glance at one another sneakily, checking each other out on the low, being a tease. You get self conscious at times but I always shoot it down with my sincerity. I have to look away quickly when I am tempted to touch your thighs so instead I just smile at you with a star gaze. You crack a large grin across your face, wide as your chinky eyes and cover your mouth in laughter and we both become ablaze. It feels like forever. You begin to play with my hair as I let my hand linger on yours, our shoulders accidently bumping and we slowly lose ourselves in this endeavor. You place a gentle finger on my eyes, removing an eyelash and blowing at it, making a wish. I suddenly feel something within me, being more euphoric than I was when I first saw you. You grab my hand and squeeze it, going for a nice walk in the boardwalk, enjoying the view and taking pictures as something between us grew. That's when you pulled me in, giving me a gentle pick on the lips as I couldn't believe what was happening. You make me feel alright, everything slows down as we both are capturing this moment. You asked the daring question before I could even say a word and I said yes without a moment stolen. A car ride later we enter a beautiful spacious room with a view of exquisite nature, bright blue skies, a strong sun still shining and lots of bright green trees. You laugh hysterically, pushing me on the bed so we can lose ourselves in oceans of each other as my heart screams in glee. It was as if we both were on fire and every loving moment felt incredible and it lasted longer than a festival. When we finally finished after many nurturing and devoted hours, we didn't want to end the day. We went for a swim at the nearest bay. You swam as majestic and swiftly as a mermaid. You taught me and rewarded me each time I got a lesson right as kisses weren't the only thing we traded. At night's end I walked you to your door safe and sound, enjoying the final moments before my return, kissing you goodnight before you attempt to fall asleep but fail because you were thinking of me. I can't look away as I'm in the Lexus, driving me back home, falling asleep nice and easy.

Exotic Mixture

Native American blood, exotic. I'll make love to you like it's a wedding night as we both become symbiotic. Marry the rich man but you'll never love him the way you feel about me. We'll be rich together,becoming money machines creatively. I'm bad for you but deep down you know I'm better and good for you. Ripped jeans, you catch me staring at the slits but I act like I have no clue. I want to touch you badly as my mouth begins to water in all the right places. I want to go animalistic and rip it open as you become less shy and feel the depth of the oasis. I want to dine in you, eating you out, giving you the fruits of my labor that bears all my aesthetics. White girl with native blood running through her veins, French lips and blonde hair, she's magnetic. I have all the good lines because you took all the curves. We'll kiss in the rain and give you everything you deserve. Have you smiling at your phone as hard as you'll be smiling to see me in person. You love it when my hair is wet, seemingly an aphrodisiac that works wonders for you and the lust worsens. I need a dictionary because at the sight of you I am speechless. I need a map because I am lost when you look at me and I become sleepless. You know what's my favorite color? The same color of your eyes, worth more than any dollar. I'll go frantic when I hear us making the bed squeak rapidly as we go in sync, breaking it in the process. I still want to wed you,bed you, coddle you, make you wet, kiss your freckles, lift your skirt up and ride each other like a horse as we make love in your dress. You may be a church girl but we can still do bad things together that feels so right. They can imitate you but they can't duplicate you because your smile is bright. Throw it back for me, mami, I'll be the MVP for this private show. It's a massive sugar rush, the day I asked if you wanted to sleep with me, you said yes and my gentle lips left strokes of color across your heart and watched it grow. I feel like you need a Hispanic papi in your life. I'm all natural and you'll love every inch of me even if I'm athletic because I enjoy kissing and touching every centimeter of you as one day perhaps you'll be my wife. You convinced yourself I'm too much for you but I think otherwise because we're an odd mix that fits perfectly together. I want you to rip my clothes off and make me submit to you because you're the boss and it's so much better. We can feel the softness of each other's baby soft skin and we will experience something we never thought we could share again even beyond that. Our bodies clashing, yours against mine, as you scratch me like a cat. I'll be squeezing oranges on you so I can lick the stickiness of the juicy flavor from your body as you giggle and bite your lip in a seducing fashion. The Gemini I thought I'd hate because I'd never think we'll release hidden passions. The Gemini that tortures my mind and I love it as she makes me hers. I'm yours. We can go several times throughout the day and night because we are like hungry vampires, feeding off each other and never getting enough as we become rough. We are the exotic mixture that's better than any drug known to man with an addictive tolerance with the perfect high.

Non Famous Poet

I remember when I was 18 and was made fun of for telling the boys I wrote a girl I liked a poem. I can remember their laughter at my failure and the disbelief because to them it wouldn't work but I still remained wholesome. They think smooth talk and acting like an overconfident jerk can get them the ladies but that can only get them so far when they act like idiots. Mental stimulus is important to match the physical traits, the art of seduction is something they don't know as anyone will leave them immediately. I just tossed my hands up in the sky because I knew they sucked, generic minded fools with nothing in their brain. Right now I'm not as famous but I prefer being wealthy mentally and economically so I can expand like the conquistadors from Spain. To all the girls I ever liked,

I'm sure my poetry made you feel some type of words. Even in my early days the rhymes and intricate style that was simple made you be thankful for the letters even if you all never felt the same but I lost the copies with beautiful verbs. I can't remember which age exactly but somewhere in my 13 year old mind something clicked. The girl that sometimes haunts me because I moved too fast and so sudden, a green eyed Nispanic with beautiful blonde hair with a name of Diana. Surely you won't be reading this now but at the time you were so amazing to gawk at, better looking than any novela actress I ever saw on the TV. A body so fine a 12 year old me couldn't resist that's worth more than any money made on Wall Street. We barely spoke and I often felt overconfident online. The days and years go by and I wrote another poem for someone else I loved which was a fatal attraction by design. I had no idea how to act because my passionate emotions got the better of my mind. Small, petite, curly black hair with small and delicate features, my heart yearned so deeply for her as she spoke as my death was signed. I was most likely 15 or 16 at the time and our conversations ran deep through the night. I can't remember the exact details but I was always so nervous and had to put everything I felt on paper because despite her short height, she lit a fire in my heart. My friends would push me to dance with her as I tried not to be awkward as she smiled and swayed with me but I can't remember my favorite part. I only remember what I felt and everything I dealt with. Young and eager, I didn't know any better but my heart grew bigger. Her name means white in Italian. The other one was from the southern part of North America and I bent over backwards wanting to be her knight on a white, magical stallion. I'm sure I was 17 at the time and I just acted impulsively as her straight red hair captured me. She was a set of twins but I only cared about her. It slowly began by November or October where everyone was crushing on her, fighting one another to get closer to her. The words came down on a sorrowful Valentine's Day next to the teddy bear I gave you with the help of a friend. You didn't see the note until your twin found it yet you didn't know until I had to bring it up. I look back and see what it meant to you at the time, wondering if you still have it and if it truly is hung up on your bedroom wall. You thanked me so kindly for the poem, being in shock because thank you just wasn't enough, according to you, for the beautiful words I can't remember. You felt the emotions I felt right there on the sheet of paper. You told me you'd always keep it near you, hanging it up your wall next to your bed with every ink filling my love on every acre. Now I can't remember what exactly I saw on you, but the little Pisces girl I can't remember is somewhere in my mind pushed back with the others. I don't think I regret much, but I regret not keeping my little love letters the most. They make the memory more vivid, as if they are recorded in a crystal ball that will take me to the cherished coast. I then became a 19 year old young man and gave a little rhyme to a girl named Arbnore. I wanted her more than anything but I clearly remember being a cocky jerk, if you're reading this you probably don't remember me but I'm still sorry. I cracked a joke about your voice when I first heard it and snickered with my friends as they slapped me upside the head and I'm sorry I ruined your merry moment. I didn't know much about you and acted out on impulse and can't recall what I wrote down but you also made my legs weak. It was awkward at first but you were quiet and cute, and when we speak I always cut you off like an idiot because I thought I was unique. I did make you laugh each time so I hoped you didn't mind. Your brown, hazel hair that probably smelled like lavender mixed with peaches but I'm only imagining things. Your tall slender body that curved around just right that it stings. Ever since then I just avoided you to avoid the embarrassment of rejection I put no effort in dealing with. After that no one was worthy of my poetry. At 23 a little ghetto Capricorn caught my eye but I think I see the pattern now. I get crushes based on looks when I thought I saw personality, maybe I did, but what do I know? I just went about my life but apparently you kept glancing at me as we spoke semi intimately. Your pale skin matching the same tone as mine with your stern blue eyes that cut through me but what did you see in me? To this day I do not know. I just remember on a cold January you held me in your skinny little arms as we hugged each other tightly for what seemed like forever. You apparently were glad you saw me because you missed me, never working the same shift as you, maybe that was an error. I don't know how it got to it but I remember your birthday, unless I'm wrong, January 6th. One day we crossed paths and I asked you in a smooth tone,"want to celebrate your birthday before your birthday?" I had no idea what I was doing as the guy behind me was surprised at the confidence and how it worked. I felt proud of myself. I finally did something right because I caught you off guard. You struggled to say sure, as you stuttered. I couldn't believe we were dating for a bit as I stayed an extra hour to leave with you. I felt as though we got close but what do I know? Maybe I did something wrong, maybe I didn't, as I tested you to see if you were in it for the money as you showed me the contrary, but I also wonder why I got ghosted without an explanation. If you weren't into dating me, why couldn't you just say so? Unless the little poem I gave you freaked you out as I remember you telling me not to get weird on you, no? Life goes around in circles as I don't know what I'm doing but with a classic goal in mind, reaching the American Dream of wealth and riches. A few more poems here and there to other people I hold dear in my heart. One knows who she is by the other doesn't, knocking me dead. Always with my heart on my sleeve, the words you see on these pages transfers my emotions with all its ups and downs, the dread. Maybe I never really liked or loved anyone and just adored the idea of it, or maybe it was just a kick to the head because I can't remember much these days. I just remember the constant delays. If there is something I remember is some of the titles that weren't really cliches. The mysterious girl with the tattoo? An untitled poem that said something about how your soul and mine belonged to one another, says who? Another one that went on and on about how much I thought I loved you and wanted to heal your inner demons you dealt with yet I couldn't find my other shoe. I sit and wonder how such emotions influenced my writing, all the books I read and tossed aside, how I have a knack to make them moist with mental injections of my words, but for the life of me it's still incomplete. Am I incomplete? What else do I have to achieve and who do I compete with?

Glow Up

You always seem to be on the receiving end of the short stick. Laying down on the couch, you relive the stressful moments but as soon as they're out, you become less sick as it all begins to click. Jotting it all down in my notepad, I am happy you are removing the boulders off your shoulders. You've been suffering way too much but little by little you're seeing the pattern you're working on. Despite it all, your heart is good and means well and you're always there to help even at the break of dawn. They can knock you down, batter you with words and prejudice but you always get up smiling. Every time I'm around you or when we talk, it's always such a good vibe and I can see that you're trying. It's nice to hear that you're getting stronger than yesterday because you are undefeated. Sometimes it's hard for you, looking lost and I tell you to follow me and I'll lead you to a path that is completed. Your soul is youthful, vibrant, energetic and I can feel the presence from miles away. You're golden even in your darkest days, glowing up with each step you take everyday. You're always the first one to offer a hand and I've always appreciated that, my heart looming with joy because you always do so without wanting anything in return. Little traits like that makes you so much more beautiful, winsome, and magnificent because your personality shines with positivity in times of adversity. You can stare down and take down the devil if he stood in the way. No one can stop you and you'll do anything for the ones you love. The daily grind is where your stunning mind lights bright with unconventional ideas to solve problems in an innovative and charming manner, fitting it all perfectly like a glove. You're showing us everyday how your fiery nature will make you swim in a drowning situation. You're golden, showing off your luminosity like a starlight that can guide an entire nation. Sometimes you catch me by surprise in a good way because you're transparent and down to earth that's honestly refreshing. Needing help even when you don't want to say it, it's okay because you're my favorite patient that's helping me in my profession, working towards self progression. You can show me the world with your tropical extroverted nature as I can show you the world in the mindful world with my reflective and semi introverted nature. You bring out a different side of me only a privileged type of person is allowed to see, which only makes it greater. From time to time I'll make sure to spoil you because you deserve it as much as the little ones. You also need looking after because you are worth a thousand suns. You need to see it through so you can powerfully rule the world exactly or even better as I taught you. You're golden. A superstar in disguise, you can walk all over the negativity no matter how constant it is, you're always going to come out on top. Self sufficient is the way you want to be but also need a safe space to lay your tired head, sleep merrily to fight another day.

$$$

Inexplicit thoughts, dollar signs in my head, all I see is green. It's 2 AM on my screen. I look at my watch to double check, I have confirmation. I turn on my computer, put on my headphones and it's time to make money on this automation. What goes up, comes down, can spike again, turn around, make mistakes and capitalize on that opportunity. Always an opportunist, I spent recklessly but I can make it back in a day. I have strange addictions and need a new high in my life so I'm looking for something only money can buy. I'm a professor, I'm a teacher, I'm an educator but during my off seasons, I plan, analyze, and I think so that you don't have to. I move items from one location into my pocket. I put the money from your pocket that'll magically walk itself into my checking account to increase my own amount. I already have over ten pieces of footwear, I already have all the clothes I want, I have all the food I want and I can't drink anymore because it just won't fit in my body. What else is money good for when all I do is have expensive hobbies? My eardrums explode when you complain that something goes wrong but that's part of my master plan, to trick you into giving me what I always wanted, what I bargained for but you were too greedy to see. I don't care for mansions, yachts, flashy cars, I just want to see my money grow and work while I sleep. I don't need perfect timing and waiting for the next crash, consistency so I don't have to peep. They say no matter how "woke" people are, they'll still end up slaves for the system and there is nothing they can do about it. By that logic, I rather become part of the elite. Why not? The odds would work in my favor, wouldn't it? Maybe we can manipulate the system or not, but those complaining about the rich and poor can see a new perspective they can try for themselves instead of talking about it. Let's take action so we can see an equal and opposite reaction.

Carried Away

I can remember the helpless day I felt slightly triggered. To hear that I get taken aback by what is said. To take it personal for some delays but during that time I haven't heard from the person in a week. Why does it bother me so much when I try to explain myself and turn the other cheek. I push it to the back of my mind because I've been here before and just not want to make it worse or annoy anyone. It still bothers me when I needed someone in that moment but of course I only had myself to take care of, being my own father to a lonesome son. I go crazy over little things but I guess I still haven't said much and I held back. I have to recuse myself from this because it's too close to home and I just have to place my bets on the racetrack. I still get angry over little things and the reactions from others, maybe because they don't feel what I feel, hear the words playing in my mind and it sickens me. It's a poison so I have to be distant even if it breaks my knee. It's not the act itself that bothers me, I understand that things don't go my way and you're busy handling things, it's that I decided to fall back and go my separate way. When I express that openly I still feel this strange uncaring vibe and I ask myself to please think before I say….say something I might regret. Only I understand through the metaphors that'll confuse people with no context of what I'm thinking and that makes me a threat. I have to bide my time and stay away because only I'm here for me. I appreciate the gesture of your offers but at the end of the day...I am only there for me. I'll disappear and come back at my own leisure. I'll recover and go back into my shell so I can find my own composure. People have left me before and it's okay, it doesn't faze me, I'll be fine. I'm my own cure and poison, my little emotions get carried away. As of this moment I don't care, I just want to pass through go like in the game of monopoly every week and collect my pay. Honestly, for now, there's not much to say and that's okay.

Shuffling Girl

A girl with good vibes, shuffling perfectly to the beat. I'm not sure where it is she came from, putting smooth ankle work and moving her feet. She kills it constantly and it blows my mind. It's entertaining and a good feeling when she dances, all in a perfect outline. It's almost as if she was doing a musical trance. It's pretty mesmerizing, making me wish I had moves like that when you dance. Everything is so united in one swoop, mixing all the dances that man has ever known. You just put any record on and you're in the zone. I don't even know you but you seem to appear on a for you page, always up for a good laugh. There's a lot of potential you have in this little hobby and you could take the world by storm every time you use that platform. You make a solid ground of concrete look like you're on ice. Every upload has a touch of spice. Your flow and rhythm reminds me of my younger days when my brother would light up the party with sick moves of his own. Every kick, every time you move your hips, you bring life to stone. Every song is a mood, vibing to smash hits, bringing up nostalgic memories. Keep shuffling and dancing, bringing smiles across thousands of faces.

Tired Soul

I never had anything real in my life. Don't trick me into illusions, please don't cause me strife. Don't keep my hopes up and make me imagine things in my mind, thinking it's real. It wasn't a big deal before. I'm not getting any younger. I need some sincerity to feed my hunger. Everyone always says that. They always say how I'll find someone for me yet I always fall flat. They say I deserve better. They say how whoever will end up with me will be very lucky, they'll even borrow my sweater. Spare me that because I don't want to hear it anymore. It becomes such a chore. Some people like to deal with things using substances, but have you ever been sober with eyes wide open to the fire? My soul is old and tired, if you're going to waste my time just walk away now and leave me alone, I have to keep myself fresh for the next buyer. There's bags under my eyes, tired of having situationships that lead nowhere with people who will not be present by next year. Another sleepless night, tired of counting cash, tired of economic victories, what's the point of being wealthy if I don't have someone to share it with, without having someone's lipstick to smear? They say those with the saddest hearts always write the most beautiful things. At this rate, I'll be a melancholic poet with his love spilled in ink, eventually drying up with no more wings. It'll be plucked and burned. There is so much I have left to work for and earn, but I'm tired of everything I've learned. It still makes me who I am and can't trade it for anything in the world no matter what. I can die with a smile with the belief I was better than the rest as my pride makes me think how they lost a real one, never knowing what true love I have to give but they never knew or had it. I'll be like a ghost that'll disappear forever and when you finally cry, hear the wind whisper my name, it'll be too late to appreciate my wit. I don't want them to hype me up and make me believe they're just saying nice things to make me feel good about myself, just let it go. Leave me in the sunlight and let me pack my ammo. There's a war coming, and it's an internal war that'll overflow.

Sweet Words

You're all alone, walking along the coast of the city. Heart heavy with my hoodie on, I walk past by you without glancing back yet you still see me, recognize me. You pull off my hoodie and see cuts on my face under my sunglasses. You ask me what's wrong but I just don't want to talk about it but I can turn it around light smoke and gases. I tell you a funny story as you laugh a little too loud, apologizing. You look at me, appetizing. Our eyes lock just for a bit and I ask you if your hands are heavy. You look at me confused as I replied, "let me hold it for you." You chuckle at the little attempt as you keep smiling at me like a weirdo, but I like it and want to share the same pillow. "Do you have a name or should I call you mine?" You hold my hand and take me for a walk, hearing the waves of the ocean that bring a chilly breeze that makes me have goosebumps across my spine. We sit on a bench, staring at the moon without saying a word. Enjoying the silence as I watch the subtle drama unfold. You look at me and ask why I disappeared for so long. "I knew you were busy and didn't want to annoy you, bother you, so I just went along with it." Your mouth curved into a frown, saying how distant I was and wished I kept in touch. I quickly turn away and flinch, this is too much. "I really did miss you." was what I heard but the actions spoke louder. I had a hard time believing this as lately I have become sour. Your hands find a way to turn my face towards you, with your thumbs caressing my cheeks. "I'm so sorry. I feel really close to you and thought about you for weeks." I'm easily influenced but I'm trying to resist it, as words make me melt and vulnerable, making me an easy prey. "Your eyes really are brown, I love them just like that. They're beautiful and chinky." I still feel the sadness but I somehow welcome it, welcome you as your dark cheeks turn red. I can feel my heart pounding as I'm fighting against it because for you I already bled. You express your anger towards those that hurt me, carefully examining the cuts at close range. The proximity is so close, our lips only centimeters away and it's so strange. You're still smiling at me as I try to keep my walls up but you somehow find a way around it, making me get butterflies in tummy again. I truly can't tell if it's me you want or what, but you're making me feel like a ten. You just hold my face in your palms and then just holding me together, I can feel your strength. I can feel it again, a similar wavelength. I want to neglect you but my arms wrap around you, having a mind of its own. I still feel like a little boy, I haven't aged but I know I matured, I know I'm grown. I feel more like myself but I still feel as if you have the upper hand but other times I do, too, and you just hold me in such high regard but I don't know if you're being honest or nice. I can feel the sincerity in your words and your expressions because not everyone can keep a good poker face. I still doubt it and wonder if this is another lesson, another person in my life for character development or if another one will take your place. I'm truly tired of these whirlwind romances that lead nowhere, I want something real. It's like you read my thoughts and confirm that it really is real, as you kiss me slowly and wipe your tears away. It's like I believe you yet I don't but I still want you to stay. Please, stay.

??

All I have are question marks in my mind. It keeps me blind. I'm trying to relax and unwind. I'm trying to be laidback but the thoughts creep back and keep me in a constricted bind. I'm trying to let go but it makes me sad and angry. What makes me more rageful and sorrowful is that others see things I'm not even portraying intentionally. My acts are questionable as well as my irrational thinking, screw this mentality. There is nothing I can do about it and wear my heart on my sleeve, it's sickly. People swear to their graves I fall too easily. That might be true, but there's another side to that, can't you see? It's not like I'm looking for love but I spend time around people that makes me wonder and takes months to form and people can't let me be. They push me toward things I avoid and it doesn't matter how much I beg or plead. What makes it worse are the little gestures and actions that make me see them in a different light. I want to kiss them just right. I want to sleep next to them and have them in my arms when I wake up in the morning, hugging them tight. I want to sing and dance like everyone else but I'm still like Batman, right? All the money in the world with no one to share the fancy, lavish life with and burning daylight. I may seem impatient on the outside, but I'm moving forward, taking my time. It doesn't make sense to ache and long for something I never had, so why is it hard to shut my trap and act like a mime? I'm doing all I can to stay afloat and go with the current but I make the current and I'm working overtime. Meditating and daydreaming. This was spoken into existence and this is just a little bump in the road, a long bump, and I won't go like a victimless crime. I've wasted money on things just to feel the high from life yet I'm still sober because I'm such a masochist, hungry for an epic meal time. I need this pain to fuel me, the dark energy that makes me achieve something greater in myself to reach grander heights because I need the dime. I can't tell what's good for me or not, all I see and hear are toxic this, toxic that, but I know I'm toxic, too, and it leaves such a bad connotation yet all I had was reproach for a long time. I cannot tell what is good for me or not, I need to climb. I'm pushing forward with obstacles hitting me in the face like the wind and I need it to maintain myself in my prime. It's difficult being absorbent to everything, just feeling and thinking. Yes, we all need healing, but it's so generic and I'm sure there's so much more but sometimes I feel like I'm shrinking. I have the stamina to prove everyone wrong, to make myself right, dust myself off and keep fighting to each end and I don't care, I'll keep digging. Even when I've lost all my strength, all my limbs, tired all the time, I'm still winning. That's not all I want, but in my upbringing I was taught to go down swinging. One day you'll see, I'll see and prove myself that I'll reach the mountain top even if I have to get there limping.

Materialistic Goals

People test me and doubt me, question me when I've shown them the path. I'm upgraded and I've already done the math. Spend money to make money, make it work for you while you take a bath. You want to be rich yet complain about how others go around it, calling it a gamble when there's research involved with an educated risk, thinking I'm a sociopath. Just relax, look at it go down, be patient and watch it rise back up like it's going on a warpath leaving a bloodbath. Thousandnaire is the stepping stone to being a millionaire. Who needs all that money when you can sit on the chair? Who went to sleep hungry and cried about life not being fair? How many times have you dipped in, trying to fight things coming at you from life like it's a wild grizzly bear? How many holes in your shoes, your pockets will it take to put yourself in your own state of welfare? It's a tough world and money makes the world go round, numbers don't lie while we do, so you have to take care. Gold chains, diamonds, don't need them, steal them and sell them to the highest bidder and hide out in Delaware. Summertime is around the corner and what are you going to do to prepare in advance? Watch out because it'll be like the purge when the crazies come out, are you willing to take that chance? Drive around in your sports car with shades and take a glance. I finally made it, a slow progress and I'm going straight to enhance. Versace, Dolce, smelling nice and fresh while you're worried about the wrong person while I'm out here doing a snake dance. Watches and bracelets, the materialistic things we don't need but looks nice on me, my style will have you in a trance. Always a romantic, I've got to keep my head up and not worry about romance. Focus on my progress, material wealth is something I can fall back on, increase my level of finance. I'm not in disillusion, I'm just pissed off, so just back off, watch me blast off. No real idol, just people I study and learn while they remain idle. It doesn't matter how many times I've been trifled, I still come out on top and have similar features of a model. An annoying cycle with sounds I hear that constantly annoy me, nagging at me, I'm just waiting for my future arrival. I'm collecting the infinity stones with motives and passions not even I can put into words, and no, I am not in denial. I've been asked a lot of stupid questions in my life, and never have I felt so annoyed when I was asked if I'm working just to pay bills or if I want to become something of myself and that question in itself is vile. I'm not running away from anything, I'm right here, and in that moment I've already had this ill feeling of being triggered because it was as if for that month you didn't hear what I said and now I'm going primal. I'm a quarter away from my goal, 25,000 is just one milestone that'll be one million in a few years, that number is vital. Yes, I'm spending, buying and breaking to set myself on fire to push me to reach the platinum vinyl. I don't need to work overtime, I've been blessed with a title. The details that were given but you still don't know me, so get ready for the reprisal. I'll rise from the burned ashes, the eternal and constant revival. It doesn't matter how low you want to put me, I'll make space to climb out of holes you want to put me in, and it'll be homicidal. The dark energy for success, it'll be a mess, take a guess, don't stress, if you're up for it I'll take your hand and teach you the process. When you laugh at it and spit at my face, I'll repress the foul gesture, I'll make all the excess as I snap my finger while you regress. I have to confess, I still want a noblesse, a queen to my kingdom but for now I have to maintain the press, show my face in the news to exhibit my assets in a formal address. Materialistic goals to this fire beat, the quiet boy who had nothing to eat, always looking neat and you'll watch the heat.

Competing with myself, I'm complete because I'm already elite, make you secrete dopamine in your brain and have you on the edge of your seat.

Retroactive

Running at the speed of sound, my body has been infected with a virus. I have been mutating over and over and I don't know what's going on...did they dunk me in the water of Lazarus? I can't tell what's going on but I can feel myself changing and I can hear them chanting, the haunting chorus. They speak in a language I don't understand, something I can't speak, yet I understand it. Finally catching my breath, I can finally see what's around me. This is an alternate world, something I've never seen this before but I remember why I came here...to steal fruit from the forbidden tree. It's as if I'm part Spider-Man and Superman, a clone made to steal for the high and mighty and as my services are paid to the highest degree. I don't remember what my suit looks like but I'm sure it doesn't look crappy. It's a dark world here, neon lights that bring this sad city to life with rain dimming it down. Everyone here wears a sad frown. This holy tree is hidden uptown. In plain view...hmm…I wonder who planted it there and thought they were smart enough and worthy enough to wear the crown. I zipped and swung my way to the destination unnoticed by everyone, creeping my way to steal the treasure, but I was met by a titan, standing taller than the empire. He reached much higher than the twin towers. He tried to light me on fire. My senses and reflexes helped me to avoid and dodge his attacks but my mission was much more dire. I blew a strong wind that made the city blue like the ice age, many eons prior. The titan could only look at me as he knew he lost, one strong punch behind my body weight, he collapsed down and I was the reason for this enchanted hire. The golden apple was the key to unlock the universe. It must be a curse but I'm the nurse that walks a fine line between killing and saving but it could've been much worse. Reaching for my time watch, I open a portal to transverse back to my time so I can add more dollars in my purse.

Rich Orphan

There once was a little billionaire orphan. He was kind and gentle but his parents always took caution. His parents were taken away by an evil person following them who wanted their fortune. One day after enjoying some ice cream in the park coming home from the carnival, they were gunned down in front of the little boy. This took away everything from him, especially his joy. This destroyed the boy as the cops quickly came to handle the mess, arresting the man with the failed master plan. They say not to take things personal with people you're not personal with, yet how can we not? Being closely attached to those who feel naught. Having money but with an empty heart. This was a heavy split up. The little boy grew up alone with no one to care for him but himself. He had bulletproof ideas he wanted to put to good use but he had no motivation to produce. Everything he touched turned to gold but nobody cared for him, the little orphan had no real friends. They only wanted his money and status of being in his circle and they didn't even try to make amends. He still tried, never pushing people away or building walls around himself. He smiled and befriended whomever he came across, even the people that beat him up for his lunch money. He fell in love way too many times, offering full services of buffets, love letters, and grand gestures but nobody paid him any mind. He slowly became as sad as the day his parents were shot and felt bitter towards mankind. He told himself that he didn't need anyone and no matter what he did, he always got hurt in some shape or form and people would always leave him and he wished he was blind. He didn't want to see the world for what it was anymore, it was too dark for him so he would rather see the eternal darkness by vision loss. He kept his feelings to himself and avoided help of any kind, always questioning any act of kindness. He wouldn't trust anything even if he held a six foot pole to poke something because he was tired of the dryness. He recovered slowly but he received the short end of the stock each time. He was tired and angry so he began drinking. Everyday after school a glass of champagne or wine. The little orphan became disheveled but made it look attractive, wanting to catch moths to a flame and he knew he became dangerous. He had his fair share of one night stands but he was tired of it. He felt so empty as he became older, never knowing real love. Ten years later he became the child version of himself before his parents died, sort of. One day this changed when he met a beautiful girl, foreign and exotic in every way possible. A cute and simple approach as he tried to be confident but he stuttered and felt horrible. Just by the look of her brown eyes, her facial features of soft cheekbones and big lips, yes, all physical but he stuttered, still. She was small and had wavy and curly hair, her style wasn't anything to gawk at but it worked, it was simple, alluring and easy to fulfill. He mustered the strength to grab a pen and paper to jot down a little line that made her smile, leaving his number on the back of her bill. Her skin was soft and a bit tan, adding some color to his life and felt warm like drinking milk with coffee. He smiled and walked away, a little shy but a little bit happy. He was a little crazy. The trauma was somewhat left untreated but he coped anyway. He didn't need medication because he still managed to pull himself through but lately...he had conversations with himself during sleepless nights. "You're crazy, I hope you know that. You sometimes act like a brat. Always judging people, aren't you? I can't help it, I'm mean in some ways yet I'm still nice, aren't I? Maybe, or is that a lie? Huh….you know, I can't tell, really. It's time to sleep but I keep thinking about her. She's new, I haven't seen her around her before. Yeah, she definitely is new and there's tons to explore. I know, but I can't help but remember the other things. Please don't...I implore you. Stop, don't you do it. I'm sorry but I can't help it." The little prince drifted asleep. He dreamt a little dream about the girl, a king maker. She was born half an angel and half human, granting the wish of the sad little orphan to no longer wanting to become a dictator. He ruled over his fairytale kingdom with his lover and his rule was as transparent as water vapor. The kingdom got on the radar of raiders who noticed the industrious progress of the kingdom and wanted to ruin their peace because they were his number one hater. There was a Great War to defend the little kingdom and before the orphan king slayed his enemy, he woke up in cold sweat. None of it was real and he's still in his own 10 year old body, dreaming of the future inside the police station without giving his report of the sad occurrence and he realized he lost the bet. The little orphan turned around and saw a devilish leprechaun flipping a coin, wanting to bet again. What was the wager? To slay the monster under the bed to live a happier life without changing the horrible events of the past, shrouding in mystery of the soon to be dark teenager.

Little Shrimp

Time and time again the little shrimp didn't listen. His outer shell has become soft and falls from time to time, he just kept on wishing. The little shrimp under the sea would meet a school of fish, joking and talking to them and became an addition to his life, something he would envision. He felt good about it but from time to time they would just overlook him. He doesn't notice it and tries to be understanding but sometimes he would get grim. The little shrimp under the sea just focused on collecting his stones, making a collection of pebbles because it seemed like being the richest in the ocean would cure his heartbreak. He shakes it off when a lobster he cherished and loved decided to drop him telling him she just needed space and break, just being one of the many usual flakes. He thought about everything wrong he did and figured she would be better off without the little shrimp. It became an unneeded chip in his shoulder trying to make up for the damage he thought he had done but didn't want to seem like a wimp. Not only was he collecting little pebbles and rocks, he was now training to get his little claws bigger. He became a digger. He found little golden nuggets and fought crabs to keep them safe in his little home. It was a constant mental nag for the little fish but he didn't lose sleep because he needed space to roam. He did everything he could but he would feel blue at times and even cry about it. He took long showers to come back from it and after a year he saw the sun lit. It shone brightly through the ocean. The little shrimp found a potion under the ocean and drank from it, a strange potion. The potion was like a drug and he began dancing. He was dancing alone, figuring out plans to distract himself from the constant nagging and continued jamming. It was relaxing for the shrimp, moving his little legs and claws, swaying his antennas to the beat and it was entrancing. He was tired of dealing with other beings, he figured he would just do the same. Other shrimps, fish, dolphins, sharks, and many sea critters saw his little party. They were fond of it, wanting to dance with him and they did but was it for pity? The poor little shrimp was just as confused but he needed barriers and boundaries. He wanted a long vacation and to disappear. He wanted peace but there were too many troubles around him and it was even the beginning of his problems in the Atlantic. He left the people dancing because his travels would begin soon, he wanted to see the fallen Titanic. He wanted to see the Pacific. He needed a breather and let go of everything and everyone, make a new chapter in his little life but he didn't want to cause panic. He slowly drifted away from everyone and only gave attention to those he deemed worthy.

Devil's Angel

An age old folklore but I am the living truth to it. My father is a devil, I'm his little angel because my mother was an angel. They called us nephilim and we were wiped out because we were too troublesome. My father is locked away in a cage and the only way I get to see him is to tempt someone to do bad things, a deal I made with the devil. I don't like it one bit but I had to stoop down to his level. My mother is sick, she is dying, losing her life force because she committed a crime, my species is not allowed to have life. My baby face makes people underestimate me heavily and this is where I come in to sleep with any wife. I'm not particular in this aspect of the deal and it hurts me more to break up marriages but my father knows how to make the special medicine. I'm very sorry, Evelyn. Your husband makes it so much easier, he abuses you in ways no human should and I always treat you right the way a proper man should. I always leave you but I fear you may end up somewhere worse than where I originally found you, so I convinced your husband to rob a bank and I gave him the perfect plan. We would have pulled off with five million dollars if I didn't fly away, calling the police to have him be the only culprit. I feel so dirty for these many betrayals and it ruins my spirit. I tempt people into doing things that are out of character and unique to them so I can have a spot at the dinner table with my father. I take advantage of people with drinking problems, those who already have already earned their chips and I pop out of nowhere as their friend who invites them out for drinks and good food, an enabler. I schedule meetings with my father, as we spend time catching up and he fills me with specific details of the cocktail. He cries alongside me but I can't tell if he actually means it or if it's just guilt, it's a good sale. I touched my father's forehead and gave him some angel energy to last for the next hour. I need to see who he is without the hardcore filters and chains, showing only a delicate flower. I go back to earth and pose as advisors for the politicians and show them a magnificent plan on how to help the needy and I turn around and whisper dirty secrets to another one so they can embezzle the funds. Ultimately it is done but I make sure he is caught by tempting a lobbyist to betray his loyalty and other incumbents to testify against one another. A few years of this I found the medicine and it is potent enough to infiltrate the godly law. My mother is on the brink of death but I took her off life support and just in time gave her what she saw. It seemed to have worked for a few months and saw my own face behind her, trickery and false hopes. She kissed me goodbye as she dissipated into thin air as I walked down the path of a slippery slope. All of this for nothing, absolutely nothing and now I might as well join my father as I know why we aren't allowed to exist. We fall from grace no matter what good we do and it's easily dismissed.

Drunk Cowboy

A middle aged man stumbles on the steps of his home, hat in his hand as he jagged his keys to open his door. How long can he keep this on for? His phone has dozens of missed calls, messages and voicemails but he doesn't care. His hair long and blond, beard blonde and grey. Eyes green but dirty bags under his eyes, always having a long day. He slips and falls on his couch with nothing to say. He picks up a broken portrait with a beautiful family on it, cutting his fingers on the class and cries himself to sleep. He wakes up from nightmares at 8 am sharp, needing a shower and some extra mouthwash to energize himself to tend to the farm but his wounds cut deep. Always having a spare can in the shower, he looks at the wall, staring into blank space and begins to weep. Heading to the farm with his hat hanging low, he brushes everyone off and minds his business. Diligent worker with parents who were immigrants. He fixes the fences, hammers down loose nails in the barn, feeds the horses, shovels manure, daily chores to keep his mind off from a time where his abusive father would hit him in drunken rage. The mother would always get in the middle but it was always much worse as the little boy became more angry with himself with age. He blamed both of them, never knowing why his father was the way he was and never truly loving them. He blamed his mother for marrying such a bum. He wondered if it was better if she left with or without the boy, at least she would have been safe. One night, the boy finally summoned the courage to fight back but as usual the mother intervened but she was knocked back, a straight way to heaven. He ran away that night, never knowing what became of his father on December 11. Years later after struggling to survive, he met the love of his life. She was beautiful, strong willed and independent. They began their little musical duo and traveled across the country and both became highly dependent. It was exciting because both of their pain was ending. They healed each other's scars, able to tell what the other was thinking and in their success they donated millions to those trapped in domestic violence. Some years later they gave birth to beautiful children, a set of twins but lord knows how they would become, tireless. The old cowboy brushed some tears away, suppressing the memory as he drove the tractor. He was still wealthy, a skilled contractor. His sadness still haunted him, making the drinking an extreme liability. The gods in heaven ruined his tranquility. It hit home because on December 11, the twins were diagnosed with an incurable disease. They died soon after and broke apart the married couple and they weren't so pleased. They couldn't get over it and he failed to take care of his wife in the time she needed him the most as he looked the other way and turned to drinking, like his father. He refused to be a wife beater and child abuser so he just left her a letter and drove off to a distant land. He always had a way with words, even if it kills him to make the last stand. He told her he loved her but she needed to be happy, to seek help because he didn't want her to be her anchor, keeping her along in a sinking ship. In this part of the story I would rather just turn away, because I can feel their pain and hope they end up together again in the future, but I can't exactly move from this trip. The old cowboy took some years in isolation, work and drink in repeat. He couldn't feel the taste of the whiskey anymore, dodging liver cancer by a bullet that gave him a wake up call as he woke up on the street. On the way home with trash bags to get rid of everything and move out again, packing his things and right on the stop light on the road in his truck, he casually glances to his left. He saw his lovely wife, grey haired and some wrinkles with age but she's still as beautiful and calm as ever. She felt like someone was looking at her, eyes watching her every move and she screamed in ecstatic rage. She couldn't make sense of it but she ran out of her sedan ready to punch him but he got off his truck, too, just holding her in his arms wanting to make up for lost time. They were still in love and prayed for a second chance to make things right this time. Good times, bad times, people change, you change, I change, but it doesn't have to be so morbid. Just listen to the song, listen to the voices, take a break if you're tired. Live. Love. Laugh. Suffering will be short term but there's a reason for it, not sure what it is yet, I've lost my memory but I watch over these people sometimes.

Fire Breather

In another universe I traveled to, there were four main continents, four different nations. They were the natural elements from the planet, the main foundations. Earth, water, fire and air. They all had their cultures, traditions, governments and had so much skills to spare. One in particular, I favored the most and became one of them for some time. The most advanced, industrial and power mongers of the four, the fire nation would become a terrorizing manifestation you would tell a misbehaving child that it's past their bedtime. Although I am sensitive, highly perceptive, sympathetic and caring to a degree, I am also emotional. This made firebending easy for me to grasp as my talents became noticeable. In their eyes, I was the legendary dragon fire breather. I was the one that could help in their uprise to absolute world dominion and I was eager. My inner rage blossomed as I became a fearsome warrior as many rose up to challenge me. Although we become vulnerable and respect one another, especially the namesake, honor and respect, there were many who questioned me and went on a spree. They wanted to steal my power. I loved these moments, I had an excuse to show myself off at the finest hour. Agni kai, a meeting held at sunset to settle a dispute no matter what rank, a one on one battle to the death. My armor plates were removed, as those were moments to prove myself to the military and had to control my breath. Tight bands around my arms in traditional military pants, I stared down my opponent who literally looked down on me. Oh, well. We would dance like dragons to honor the fire lord, and the loud bang of the bong would excite my bloodlust. My enemy shoots flames from his fists, kicking a few more thrusts of fire but I shrug it off like a speck of dust. I shoot flames from my feet, accelerating like a locomotive, picking up speed and aiming head fast like a rocket. This catches him off guard as I turn my wrists around, palms facing him and shoot a wide sized flame burst. He struggles to keep up with the sheer strangers but summons willpower to reimburse. I saw the hatred in his eyes, he wanted to kill me as he shot more fireballs, trying to blind me with the brightness of his flames and attempted to spit at my eye. I was nearly burned but the anger in me flourished, turning my orange flames to bright blue, as more flashy kicks and punches confused him, overpowering him and frustrating him. I kicked him on his groin and snapped a knee cap with the same foot. He fell down and was at my mercy. I shot flames from my fist and mouth, swaying to my victory as I did the final deed, the last thing he would ever see. I burned him to a crisp as the crowd cheered. Too many of these and it became all too easy. I rose to the ranks and one by one, village by village, we exerted our law even though it was sleazy. People recognized our ships, our grand Air Force, at the mere sight of us they would cower in fear, some even puke. The nervousness we could all sense, the crippling anxiety on their faces as we took hold of their dukes. They would fight us but ultimately fail. Out power rises with the sun, the earth's core and any comets flying by. There was one emperor from the water nation who would forever hold a place in my wicked heart and I was already cocky. It was dawn with the moon still shining on the ice glaciers. He used ice cold water to trap my body as he laid many swings on me and forgot what I was even doing, what day it was. He almost broke my nose with his elbow until I regained some composure and spat little fireballs at him. Taken aback, he put out the fire and in that moment I head butted him, being free as I lit my body on fire on a whim. Nobody ever saw that before from a fire bender, as my flames became burned bright in a rainbow like color, shooting it from my body towards him as I yelled like a caveman. I had no love in my heart, only ambition to rise to the top and even become fire lord because I can. This would be part of my secret plan. I calmed down my energy and channeled it, removing emotion and turning my flames into lightning and struck the emperor, causing a heart attack. The jolts shocked him, too much energy, the bright blue electricity overworked his organs and I wanted his head on a plaque. The fire nation consumed me and changed who I was. I liked it. I told the people that they rise with the moon, as I rise with the sun. Perfect timing as dusk eased up into a bright, cold morning. Only the future will unfold slowly to the day I become ruler of this world. These people lacked vision and I guess one can say I was out here to guide them.

Lose Me

I'm not always trustworthy. I'm not always positive, my words are like a sword. They say guns and bombs are the most dangerous weapons of mankind. I say it's my mind, and I'm sorry I'm not always kind. I'm sorry if my words cut you up, it was just a moment of anger. The most dangerous part of me is my mind and I don't always speak it, I let it linger. I hold back and don't express it, only escaping with my words. I don't mean to disappoint it's just how I am, with all the raw emotion and feeling,

sometimes it's blurred. It is said people want more friends yet they push away the ones they already have. It's ok, I get it, I probably do the same if I'm stuck on my mind, too. It doesn't make it any better. I still feel what I feel and delete the messages because it's not you I want to get angry at or me, it's the situation that's beyond our control. No matter. I'll fall back because I can't harbor anything negative right now, but it hurts sometimes because I still feel cast aside while I silently shatter. It's a nuisance I feel in me. Why is it that I am praised by people I haven't spoken to in years but when it's someone I feel close to, I can't even get a little reaction of positivity? No acknowledgement, like it's nothing and I've already felt this way before. I'm sorry. Maybe I'm the rudest
one, a hypocrite who makes people see one side of me. Maybe I'm tired of holding on so I'll disappear for a bit. Drive away to California to manage a hedge fund, to gather investors and make something beyond me. I'm sorry. I know the words I use against you can make you feel some type of way. Sometimes I feel like I'm an animal that only knows how to react and not control anything, missing the balance of disrupted equilibrium. This wasn't even supposed to be about you, it's supposed to be an apology I can't even word correctly as I sit alone in my condominium. You can't make a few millions without losing friends first, call me a Judas, a genius, a monster, an enemy. I'm a punk and I deserve your anger without empathy. I'm sorry for saying what I said yet I felt what I felt. Maybe there's no way you'll forgive me, maybe you will, not entirely sure but I'm ready if you want to use the belt. I won't cry,I won't flinch, I won't fight back. I'm a good soldier, I try to keep it to myself and when I complain I get judged first, get cut off, interrupted without being able to tell the full story. It's okay. Others do listen first, it's fine, I'm a good soldier. It doesn't matter. I still get support regardless if it's not from you so I have to mind my business and march on forward, like a toy soldier. I'm not trying to advertise much, I'm saying what my truth is and what I feel, so if you wouldn't want to be next to me I get it. I wouldn't want to be near me either, but there's still room for growth because I've been here before. I turn back and see the sunset hit the skylight, shiny wooden floors with white walls, long sofas around and I've finally made it. Taking another sip of my moscato, it brings back some memories that are somewhat painful to handle. It'll get better with time, just avoiding the situation and pushing it behind my brain.

High School Story

New kid from the block, curly, blonde brown eyed baby faced boy. He was shy but tried to hide it behind confidence trying hard not to annoy. On his first day to school, he took the bus. Feeling awkward in the crowded place, he took a seat next to a redhead and tried not to make a fuss. He dropped his jaw in awe because she was the most beautiful person he has ever seen in his life. Natural red hair, dark red lipstick and freckles to match her dark blue irises. She was quiet but rolled her eyes at him, as he tried to be polite but he stuttered and began sweating as if he had multiple viruses. He lost his cool and was nervous, heart beating so fast he became dizzy. If she doesn't make me stutter I don't want her. I know the feeling, all right. She was staring lifelessly out the window as he kept glancing at her while looking down. Skye. Skye was her name, something she said quietly. "Oh, to meet you nice. Um...nice to meet you." He turned red and glanced away, biting his lip because he acted stupidly. The girl giggled but didn't say anything. One stop away, the boy just got up and walked to school, a bit embarrassed but didn't notice he dropped his ring. She noticed it on the floor, picked it up and admired it. It held a family crest name on it, a giant sapphire rock engulfed in black metal. An heirloom. The curly haired boy shuffled around, bumping people in the hallway as he grabbed the first seat in his class only to find out he was in the wrong one. As the other kids laughed at him, he rushed out the door and ran to his algebra class. No seats available in the front as the teacher shot the boy a dirty look. He pulled his hoodie up to cover his embarrassment and took an empty seat. As he removed his hoodie he noticed Skye looking at him but turned away quickly to hide away the blushing heat. She passed him a note with his ring on it, saying how he dropped it and should be careful next time. He thanked the redhead and went about his day. He sat alone outside, enjoying the September sun in the chilly warm atmosphere. He heard a loud clunk next to him, to his surprise it was the mysterious girl and he looked like a deer staring at headlights. "You act like you've never spoken to a girl before. What's your name, blondie?" The boy stuttered but cracked a smile, saying everyone calls him Jorgi, but spelled in the Portuguese way. She glanced back, not meeting many foreign people in her day, asking him where he's from. He opens up and tells her stories from his child vacations in Brazil and his family. She laughed at his stories and little misfortunes, something she doesn't really do. You see, she's reserved and doesn't have many friends at all, always a loner. She's from a rich family, the most hated one in the town, but she managed to keep it a secret before it's over. They exchange numbers and talk all the time. They get close day by day, both being excited and happy when they hear their phone chime. One day she comes from behind, covering his eyes as she asks the classic line, "guess who?" It didn't take two seconds for him to know who. He grabbed her hands and began kissing her fingers, her knuckles, her hands. She blushed and pulled away quickly, unsure of what happened and why she enjoyed it as her heart expanded. She sat next to him and leaned her head on his shoulder as he wrapped her gently in his arms. He fixed her hair, tucked a loose piece behind her ear, staring longingly at her and kissed her, finally, without raising any alarms. Her eyes shot wide open but she relaxed, her first time kissing a boy that wasn't actually out for her money. Returning the passion, puppy love, she kisses him back more and more and none of them felt anything funny. They hugged each other as the little action spoke louder than words. A little romance to fill the world with something positive, as I fly back to my condo with a little joy. Good job, kid.

I Don't Know

I don't know, I don't know, I don't know. Why do you ask me for help if all I do is get you angry and put on a show? I feel so goddamn useless, asking something way beyond me yet when you do some mistakes you don't get yelled at? What am I supposed to do with that? Making me feel like I'm 12 again, a retarded youngling with no knowledge of the outside world, lacking the experience. Putting me in a bad mood, always so serious. Always helping you out when you ask for it, asking how high you want me to jump, happy to do it and the reason why is mysterious to me. Is it love or is it loyalty to the one that birthed you? Sometimes I feel like she loves you more than me but I shake it off yet this is what I feel in the rear view. I look at myself in mirror, feeling stupid and useless. I give you all the help and love, maybe because I feel bad, but now I'm clueless. No pressure, this is you, this is me, always sentimental over the little things and now I take the bullets for you, willing to die for you because you're the one with more to lose. I have no one, just take the pins to my accounts, use my wealth and tell the ones I hold dear to me I love them. Break my heart again, pick up the pieces with tears in my eyes, sacrificing everything I ever accumulated for you and even though you love me back, it doesn't always feel that way. Always the step son, step brother, I hold it in because I get angry. Am I mad? Am I wrong? Do I really care or do I love your spawns more than you? Shifting my brain daily, maybe I'm crazy. Ignoring you isn't always easy. I don't have any vendetta, it just builds up, the little things and you make me question everything about me. I'm getting older now but you always make me feel like I'm a little boy when I'm with you, so no, keep my guard up even more with you because I don't really know you. I just know how you are but we don't know each other, strangers with the same mother. It'll get better. Waiting for them to die, maybe I'll displease you and disappear, never hearing from me again. Deuces, take my wealth, take my spirit over sensitive over things that don't have to make sense. Remove the safety, you won't ever see me, meet my wife or see my little babies. Deuces, no money or brain to help you when you need it. Good luck to the ones I love, deuces. You'll never see me, maybe, good luck finding someone else who'll be part of your muses. See my name on that statue? Even after I'm long gone you can go ahead and cry with regret, I don't even care anymore. I'm sorry, maybe I'll resent you a little more. Maybe I won't. Maybe I'll shift my grudges and hold it closer to my heart, make you believe I'm over it. I don't hate you because I'm always trying to protect you as if you're the younger one. I don't know, I don't know, I don't know, just tired of being the one to be your punching bag, always taking the run. It's ok, maybe I'm wrong because I never know what you're thinking. I feel like I'm always sinking. You hated me for being born, then you got over it but I'm sure I took your spot and it'll linger in your subconscious. You tell me to live my best life but I can't right now, I need to recharge and when I see the bottles of liquor, I always remember the goddamn weekends you put us through. I remember the overnight worries, the day you died on that table and he didn't care, while we cried as the doctors pumped your heart back to life. I don't know, I don't know, I don't know, it took you long to change for the better but you always treat me like an old service dog. I never say anything and I never will, I don't need to drag you down like a hog. Pull up my rags, I'll deal with it on my own terms and just keep tabs.

Red Witch

Sitting on the roof, enjoying the summer night sky. Staring at the moon is
much easier than staring at the sun because you can play "I spy with my
little eye". It shines brightly but doesn't have to burn the sensitivities. I
look down at the little villa, people walking around enjoying their time
alive. I look to the side, remembering a girl who used to sit with me. "Do
you miss it?" Miss what? "The first thing that came to mind." She would
always dig deep into my thoughts to the little parts I declined. The initials
that go together, it rhymes with you and I. She would ruffle my hair, push
the loose hairs behind my ears and kiss me and I knew I was a lucky guy. I
did a little magic trick and pulled a little blue rose from her ear, the rarest
on the island. We danced and sang on the rooftop, drinking and having fun
on the highland. Her hands slipped sensually on my waist, as we had long
conversations. Sometimes we enjoyed the silence, enjoying the serenity
and hearing each other's silent breathing, holding the passionate desire in
reservation. You would tell me how you wanted to trace the scars from my
back and try to heal them with your magic. You were a gifted witch and
that was fantastic. You would make the objects move and dance along with
us in perfect rhythm. You would wrap a yellow snake around your neck
and seduce me nightly that blurs up my vision. We would stare at the
mirror, a reflection showing a light skin girl, with beautiful, soft red curls
and eyes as blue as a sapphire. She would like to play with my light stubble
and pretend I'm a pirate and playfully calling me a liar. Placing a finger on
my lips, kissing my cheeks and singing to me as I was caught off guard
with a sweet surprise. She would light the candles with magical
blue flames and changing the color of the room to iridescent, something
difficult to fantasize. She would be with me, filling my brain with lullabies.
She promised marriage with babies to come, manifesting our love and joy
into living beings that would hopefully carry and pass down the love
through generations. That's when the French colonizers came and burned
everything down. I didn't know where she went but I couldn't find her but
her burned nightgown. I found a letter, still fresh with wet tears on it. She
said she became a moon spirit so she can help those that died to find peace
but wished she could split herself in two just to be with me but she already
knew...she knew I was strong enough to walk this earth without her no
matter how blue my heart would become. So now when I look at the night

sky on the night of a full moon, I see you. In the little villa, a home I wouldn't want to call home, I remember you from the pre-revolutionary era all those years ago. I still miss you. I still wonder about you. My little red witch.

Artificial Feelings

I don't like going down, I love it when I keep climbing up. Always curious about the future, wanting to see the new technology so I can make a backup. I wonder if I can make new friends with an AI. What is it that you imply? I want to rewind to see what I've missed from my experiences and memory. Day in and day out, comparing myself to a future version of myself, I can't remember what I held on to past memories. What was I like back then? May you please remind me? I kept my guard up for so long I don't remember if the defense mechanisms are just that or a genuine part of my DNA, part of my personality. Staring at how people talk in a civilization, ruled by the elites I know I will become a part of in the upcoming future but still an outsider. I don't fit in anywhere, I'm a different case and like a chameleon, I change personalities to adapt to the environment, always trying to be better. I know what time it is and I'm the collector. Maybe I'm a cyborg myself, a clone of the person I was made to be the spitting image of, someone that died long ago. Who is it that you borrowed from? Am I really me or am I just like the snow? Thinking about the stupid things I said, not recalling if it's a dream or if t was reality. All I care about is the money, closing my heart and altering goals to see how it can benefit me in the long run, actually. Artificial feelings to be polite, making myself an actual faker to avoid battles to a pointless war I already won. In my mind, I have no idea what's going on. Maybe it's the programming in my system unless I'm delusional trapped behind four cushion walls. I promise I'm not a junky for heroin or any hard drugs, I'm a junky for success. The present is what causes stress. Daydreaming about the future doesn't and each day I worry less. I don't age regularly, even when my hair turns grey. There was a poster on the wall saying if she's important to me show her, what's hard about that? That's the thing, I can always show it from all the angles but if they don't see it or act on it, the ball's in your court now. Artificial feelings to block out what is going on mentally, causing me to raise my brow anyhow. Get in the back of my limo, telling my driver to take me away to a different city. Packed bags in the trunk, staring out the window with flashing lights dimming in the distance as it always does eventually. A bucket of ice with champagne in it, I grab a glass from a holster and drink away as the driver picks up speed. Farewell, little city. I'll be heading west. I got tired of the east. I'll probably come back in a hundred years to see how you've fared. Maybe I won't remember any of this. Let's see what actually is real, staring out at the orange sun set across the moon, past the buildings into another time zone. I'll be all alone. I'll be alone with new people who'll join my circle as I turn to stone because I'm confused to the bone.

Knowledge

To the man who made me, I see you in me indirectly. We like the same music, we sometimes talk and act the same, don't we? Wasn't around much there mentally. Everything I know now, for the majority, I learned it on my own, didn't I? I was just introduced to it vaguely. As I got older, I became bolder. Now with this power of information I try. I try to share it with those older and younger than me. There's power in numbers. There's a cult I saw on tv, sometimes enlightening that plays in my mind while I slumber. "Take what is offered and that sometimes must be enough. The true strength of the wolf isn't its fangs, speed and skill. It's the pack. Inspire loyalty, build a pack." It's this mindset that sometimes lets me move away from being a loner, sometimes I have to sleep with an eye open but not when I have someone watching my back. Even from a distance, I can touch your mind and open a third eye. I walk this earth, sometimes alone, always learning, always growing. There was a writing on the wall in this abandoned building I was exploring. It talked about how some people talk about suicide, how they don't really want to die but they want what's killing them inside to die, to stop. If you throw yourself in the ocean and struggle to survive, to try your best to not drown, does it mean you truly want to live? This has to be something decisive. That's the little message it had, something to ponder on, food for thought. Some people tell me they don't plan to live that long, sometimes they just get tired of living entirely. Although I will miss them, I can't see that for myself. I want to live, I always live in the future in my head, I want to see that light at the end of the cave. I carved myself through mountains and parted the sea to get where I'm at. I can't tell if I'm the same because I know I'm not, but in the eyes of the beholders I didn't change. Change is good, but to them it's like I never morphed into something different, just smarter. Maybe it's time, distance, and to them I'm the little boy they left behind but now I'm farther. When you meet me at different points of my life, I'll impact you differently. When I was younger, frail and innocent, I might have been too good for this world and people would think I'd be broken by this world. Meeting me in my early 20s, you'll see some shade of innocence shaved off by a few bad years but kind hearted all the same. Meeting me in my mid 20s I might as well have killed the Cookie Monster and become the boogie man in his name. I don't know what it is you see but put the blame on me. In my early 30s I'll be at peace again, but by my mid 30s will it all have been in vain? Fast forward to a few centuries later, patterns that shift in a cycle to a man of disdain without hope for a future. Shave off another decade later and I'll be hopeful again. Knowledge, experience, that stays with you no matter how you feel on the inside. Defense mechanisms hiding behind masks I can't show, masks I take off in private, I can't tell who I really am. I just make a wish upon a shooting star in the rain as the itsy bitsy spider spins a web, crushed by my small hand. Does my youthful face hide the scars entirely? Take my shirt off and my back might show the burns and wounds from fighting giant daddy long legs from other dimensions, leviathans, all types of monsters from the upside down where NASA says we age in reverse. Living for such a long time can be a curse. The worst part is not remembering everything as it gets worse.

June Lady

Hello, there, what is it you are looking for? I know today is your birthday, the day of the four. I've brought you a little flower, I picked it out from a tree, you see. It's a daisy, and no, they don't always grow from trees but this one is special. It's nice and warm, the spring between a few days of summer, but be careful. The sun's rays are especially hot this time around but I'm sure you'll tan beautifully. I know you hate birthdays but it's okay, it's still a special day. 10 years after you turned 17, eyes still green and you're still strong and lean. No, you're not weak and puny, your mental state is growing stronger by the day and I know you love nature so I got you a little house by the ravine. We can spend days gathering berries, apples, picking off dandelions on a windy day and make a wish. I can make you breakfast and bring it before you awake, and no, it won't have steak. This won't be fake. It's been some time now and you still look as beautiful as ever, and no, it's not just your looks or the dopamines that affect me chemically. It's the bond and time we spent, it's the little frustrations that can be overlooked but backed up with understanding, it's a soulful attraction, it's the amenity. We make each other's day better. It's the countless words in my letters. Whether they are bitter or whether they are sweet, little fiery emotions I feel, overshadowed by the good memories of the special times. I look at you and you're always on my mind at times, even if I get drunk while adding lime. I sit behind this tree hearing the splashes of the river, hearing your voice in my ear, the voice I love so much to hear. Once upon a time we both said although it's sweet to make love to one another, the passion is remarkable and very different, something we never felt before it isn't entirely about the physical attraction. It's between the cuddles and hand holding, but also deeper than that. It's the simple things, the little things, sleeping in the same bed next to each other, close, cuddling as an excuse because the window is open letting chilly air come in. There was a chemistry building through time as we got to know each other, becoming closer than never before, something you said you've missed during the time gap. There wasn't a day I haven't thought about you through the tears and sore throats of pain, we were like glue even after taking several naps. Maybe I'll outlive you because I'm not from this world, always remembering to bring a daisy to your grave, washing the stone and leaving little letters and love notes here and there. I'll have something to remember you by, even after eternity. You pick up the feathers of my broken wings and place it in a jar I've kept for you, the love that may have gone by and resurfaces, healing us just a little bit. Just wanted to wish you a happy little birthday, the bond stuck to us and was growing stronger as it was sunlit. You always think I'm nuts but I can't tell, really, and you don't see how. I don't always have to bow before you but sometimes you do have a little scowl. I always make you smile though, and I want to kiss you before I die because I'm leaving tomorrow. I have a mission, a little campaign because there's a war in heaven I have to stop, so give me time and luck to borrow. I'll be back. My name is a promise on your lips and yours will taste like sweet plumper lip gloss. I can't stay away from you and when I leave tomorrow it'll be my greatest loss. I know

I also make you feel little butterflies in your tummy. Now isn't the time to get sentimental because as you're reading these words I can bet $100 you're smiling like a dummy. The little house by the ravine, June bug, it's a wondrous little place that does make fairy tales endings true, even if you hate them. Deep down living in one always makes you smile, crying happy tears because you know it's true. Perhaps I'm getting off topic, but you hate physical gifts so an emotional and intangible one will always be kept closer to your dying heart. You move me and nothing can take this from me, nothing can tear it apart. Maybe. I can wipe those tears away, I don't mind. Even if I am a killer, a conqueror and a colonizer, you don't make me feel like a monster. Most days you make me feel more human than ever. Happy birthday. I'll kiss you after I'm done admiring you in that beautiful summer dress, stroking your hair just the way you love it. I'll give you gentle pecks down your neck and shoulders. I'll spoil you rotten with my tender care. I'll find a way to carry you to bed, I know I'm strong. We don't have to let go, we can take it to the next level, as we can't say no to each other. We are safe together, even if I'm idealistic while you're realistic. Happy birthday, it's going to be fantastic.

Snake In My Living Room

To the man who raised me, you make me absolutely hate you. You used to hold me as a baby, even when I cooed. It doesn't matter how much I love you, I'm counting off the days until you die. Let's be honest because I'm not going to lie. I don't know how long it'll be, waiting patiently even if it kills me. Mixed feelings in my heart, I still love you but the way you act towards her doesn't sit right with me. All she does is care for you while you disregard her and treat her like she's your slave. You'll be on your deathbed regretting everything as I stand silently above you, with or without tears falling down my face I'll stare down at you even if you behave. I'll lock my eyes into you, taking all the willpower I have, watching them go lifeless staring back into mine. You'll be leaving this world and I'll be confused as I sign. Putting an end to a legacy you left behind. Your temper is the worst and we all have inherited from you, like a toxin running through our veins. You can't wipe off blood because it's inside us, now we have to release the chains. There are days I am disgusted to be called your son. I look at you with contempt with everything you have done. Who am I to judge? I am the son of the devil, after all. Your day in the sun has run its course but I still am not sure if I'll have a ball. Just like the other one, I have more bitter memories of you than good ones. It would be easy to look at you now, well and strong, staring you down face to face and say I hate you. You still act like an animal, an untamed beast that never leaves his cage, making others turn blue. We can't put the beast down in this world, it's completely illegal. Harmful thoughts I must tuck away for I will be banished to a deeper ring of hell, one not discovered by man in the sacred gospels. You are the snake in my living room, the dragon with many heads. No matter which one I cut off, another one grows back. Luckier than most men, you aren't hanging by multiple threads. You have everything you need at your feet and I'm always at awe at how easy you have it compared to many. I don't care if you say you are mentally unwell, I don't care how low your spirits are, you've had it all and even more until now. You lack compassion, basic understanding and even some humility. You preach about the gods and how the mortals should behave yet do you really act the same? My own lack of action is the other half that rationalizes better judgement because I cannot let out my own beast given to me by your seed. I refuse to be anything like you while the other two are slowly becoming just like you. It doesn't matter how sharp my sword is, you are impenetrable with your thick skin and thick head. I cannot get through to you, not even with your black heart. I will defy everything in my nature that resembles you. If I become the thing I hate the most, I will send an army to kill me because I never want to become anything like you. I have to be better. I need to be better. I cannot be like the snake in my living room. Unless it's too late and I'm in over my head that I cannot see past myself in the reflection of you. I hate you. I loathe you yet I still love you. I've always known where I have inherited my evil heart from, I already knew deep down inside it's from you. It doesn't matter how many internal struggles I have, you're not to blame entirely because I'm grown now, yet you still have the heavy influence on me. It's a shame. Maybe I truly am just like you, a snake.

November

I won't share your secret entirely. Your birthday...it's the day after my mother's. Don't worry, I won't be long to bother. You're mysterious and intense, very subtle. You're always on the grind, hard on the hustle. I want you to take it easy, relax with me, enjoy a little dinner with some sweet Sauvignon. It'll be a summer time breeze in a far away land, even if it's cold in November in most places, I want to hear your opinion. The way you do things, there's a method to your madness. You go a little coo coo because there's a lot on your mind, I want to teach and give you my calmness. I want you to let go, so on your birthday I'll give a little piece to you. You're like the beat of this music, this song, jumping and jumping from place to place, thought to thought, I'll teach you something new. You can let go with me, take my hand and act silly together in the bright moonlight. Look up, stare at the stars because you are one. I can make a constellation of your smile up there, you can kill me with your sexy look and not with a gun. It's those eyes...those eyes that pierce through my soul, send shivers through my skin, control the rhythm of my heart beat, destroy my pulse. I try not to act on impulse. You can dance with me, but you don't want anyone to see. Not that you're embarrassed but you're so damn secretive, clouding up yourself with smoke and mirrors. You're a killer. Not in the homicidal sense, no, it's how you draw people in even the ones you don't want to make time for. What is it about you that I like? Why do I see myself in you? Why do they keep mentioning it every so often? You don't mind having me around so close, do you? A little gift that catches you by surprise, not very easy to do, but doable nonetheless. You're a November baby and I can see myself being happy. With you, we are the perfect water sign team. Without you I have to learn to cope being a one man army, so it may seem. We can run along the coast on the beach of the villa, taking a little swim in the ocean. We can take a little boat in the Mediterranean Sea. We can ride on top of the Loch Ness monster and show the world we are champions, maybe. My gift to you is to ease your mind, let you gather your thoughts and stop the flow of your river that floods a dam. I am your watergate, I can ease your troubles and take care of you since you told me you can barely take care of yourself. You always smile at me but what do you truly see? I can hide it all behind my innocent pretense but I know you see right through me. I'm always puzzled by your gestures and voice tonality. For your birthday, as far as you may be, far down the line in the future, I want you to know I remember you. It's a date I'll hold as close as mine only with more significance. There's this uneven pressure, an unspoken tension until the moon shines brightly on your face, as it rains and pours you give me a gift on your birthday. You kiss me. You kiss me like never before, like never anyone has, this time you don't actually stab me like a black widow but you sting me differently because you're a scorpion. It's not poisonous, no, but it's toxins of your emotions that you hide behind your anger, it's glorious. A secret scorpio, but deep down inside you appreciate my thoughts of you, my remembrance. Sometimes you'd forget your own birthday but I want you to feel special and loved on that day. It won't be long now, just a few months ahead during the fall. You'll be shocked when you receive my call. Intertwining timelines but we are still there, both alive and well, young or old, eternal youth, just holding a shy gaze with a wholesome smile. Even if I'm always frowning, when you look at me I can't help but smile. Calling you beautiful would be an injustice to a given fact, calling you merciful would be putting you on a pedestal. You are a million things to me, one in a million chances, a special being of many I hold in my heart. Today is just for you and I. I've controlled my nervousness around you but have you always been caught off guard by my silly ways and mannerisms? Does my intelligence always brighten up your day and relieve your stress? Am I the problem solver you've been looking for, the answers you sought but never knew until I walked in the room? I wanted to place my hand on your shoulder as you looked up at me, as if you were a little girl and I'd be a protective figure yet you are older than me. Maybe you're the one that does the protecting. A youthful smile that makes me break a sweat because I'm always so quiet and stern, a strict look of disdain towards the general population. Even when I get annoyed and roll my eyes, I don't understand why you deal with me and make my life easier, helping me. That's why I want to return your gift, kissing you back softly, gaining control of your mind and using it against you passionately. Maybe it's a lot to deal with, maybe it's not. November baby, will you be my equal to my June baby? You've been on my thoughts again lately.

Lightning Storm

Thunderstorms, lightning strikes. It's 2020, are you here to take my life? It was energized by the sun. It was the most horrifying thing I have ever seen, something beyond natural. My brother was in tears, saying that whatever happens, if we die, he'll always love me and he was sorry. I didn't believe what was going on entirely, I was shocked, but I knew when he said that I had to worry. Lightning zapping through violently, destroying buildings and zapping anything in its path. I saw it destroy the structure of a titan, the building just collapsed as if it were made of cardboard. This was a vivid nightmare. For the first time in my life, I felt actual fear. It goes beyond everything I ever saw and went through, it goes beyond dodging bullets and being impaled many times over. It was incomprehensible, much scarier than my father's rage, something older than a sage. I saw a man get burned and melted right in front of me when he got struck by lightning. I saw his limbs fly, I saw the scar on his face, disgusting. This was worse than staring down a dragon face to face. Even at night when I survived , the moon wasn't as strong but some lightning was still around, but not striking anything. It was raging around it, high in the sky. I don't remember what happened next but I luckily woke up from this nightmare, just barely. The storm, the thunder claps, the lightning, the rage I feel inside for so long I thought was tucked away and forgotten. It is internal and it's rotten. I always feel some type of way over something I don't understand. This will go as planned. The manifestation of my subconscious, walking out in the dark city with heavy rain. It's an invasion of my pain. The anger, the unyielding rage, I am the lightning. I am the one that burns, melts, destroys, in an instant and it's frightening. I am not sure what I am capable of anymore, I see a face that's not mine in the puddle, as the face stares back at me. It stares back at me and I see the evil, all I want to do is run free. I want to be someone else but my screams of violent roars shake the earth, forming thunder shocks and heat around me. I must be crazy. I appear vicious, no amount of riches can change me, maybe it does but it's overshadowed but what's soon to be followed. It's irrelevant, nothing truly benefits, I forgot my etiquette and like a supernova I explode in astonishment. I am the lightning. I am the curse. I am the destroyer that brings fear through my anger, I'm trying my best to not make it worse. I've already taken so much and I don't need anymore.

Simple Things

The simple things in life aren't always easy to come by. It's cliche to say I'm not a regular guy, somewhat shy, but we can give this a try. When I'm building walls around me, I hold my arm because I can't think straight.

Take a little walk in the summertime, laughing and talking, eating ice cream until it's late. Always looking down but I've got to keep my head up. You cusp your hands on my face and kiss my nose like I'm a pup. It's all sunshine and rainbows with you. It'll be easy, maybe, but I'm crazy so I'm not sure if we can fit the other shoe and I get distracted because I love the smell of your shampoo. You ask me for help but your mind wanders. You glance away when I look at you, smiling at each other makes me go bonkers. You get up from your chair, teaching me what we're going to do today, brushing shoulders without care. I side step away but move closer because your skin is soft and cold, not wanting this to be over. You ask me questions that make me think long and hard, analyzing everything because it's just how I am if I care too much. In this bubble, in my mind, you create a safe space. I can feel what I feel without judgement or fear repercussion, even when I say something stupid and you make a face, it's no problem and no need for a discussion. We don't have to change each other, change our ways, how we think, usually similar yet quite different. You're free in the ways I am not, while my mode of thinking is sometimes more free in some of the ways you are not. Even in the silence there's no pressure, enjoying each other's company without fear of judgement or a careless thought. I love the sound of your laugh, the way your smile creates wrinkles on each side of your mouth. It's all the little details I notice but I can't say them outright, I might get in trouble and get locked up in the south. I don't ask for much, just a full day with you under the hot summer sky. Enjoying a picnic in the park in sweet July. You can tease me as I make jokes, laughing so hard to the point it's difficult to breathe. You can kiss me goodbye but I don't want you to leave. Laying down, holding each other a bit too tightly, we enjoy the sunset pink sky. The clouds look beautiful and moving slowly. You ask me what's the worst thing I have ever done but I don't want to answer that. Instead I turn the carnage into another story, filling the gaps of something less bad because I don't want you to see how horrible I can be. You're so good at it because you've seen right through the lie but you say you don't blame me. Everyone's done a little bad. You tell me the whole story of the past wars and horrible sacrifices I ever had. You share some of your dirty secrets because you say you trust me. Everybody always does, I just have that face and personality people feel comfortable and safe with. Why? You tell me not to worry, I'm only human but I'm not, not really. You make me love transparency. The simple things I hold on to, the way you make me feel can't just go away.

Midnight Thoughts

You're from the future, I'm from the past. Maybe you think I'm being dumb but honestly I'm just numb. Who would your beautiful mother be? How many years into the future will I see you? Midnight thoughts have me thinking about my children, what they would be like, what kind of person they'd turn out to be. I recall naming one Luna if it would be a girl but I'm still clueless what name I'd give a boy. Do you have my wavy, thick black hair or your mother's? I wonder what hair color you might have, would it be like your brother's? Marrying your mother would be the first after falling in love with her. Not sure who'd she be but I know I'd spoil her with fancy fur. I'd still look so young, I barely age, I'd probably look like your older sibling next to you. Would you be arrogant being born into wealth, little one? By then you'd inherit our traits and we'll love you more than anyone. I'll love all three of you but I hope you wouldn't think less of me because of my past. You see, your father has lived a long time and has been a warlord, a conqueror, a destroyer, a savior, a healer, a colonizer. There have been so many things I have done, both good and bad, but I'd be wiser then. You'd be half of me, a demon and an angel, and half of what your beloved and cherished mother would be, a full on angel in human form. She saved my life, you see. She's everything I ever wanted and more, she loves me back just as much, she loves me harder than anyone ever let me, allowed me, reciprocity is all I searched for and she was there. Like two peas in a pod, individually being happy but with her we make each other happy. Almost too happy that it's hard to believe and it's all sappy. We all can't get enough of each other and I know you'll grow up in a loving home. You won't fear us, you won't hide anything from us, well maybe you will, all kids do, lord knows I did. You won't be alone. I know somewhat what it's like to have kids. I've cared for so many, never really knowing if I raised some indirectly. I love you. You'll be the epitome and manifestation of our love, flexible and strong like a bamboo. You're both heirs to my throne. Perhaps you might even be my little clones. You will rule this earth with everything I've shown. You'll be better equipped for this harsh world. Maybe you'll be as emotional as me. If you are, I'll give you some of my good luck because we will experience it differently with hypersensitivity. You will feel deeply, hurt profoundly, love immensely, hate ardently, always have this internal struggle with good versus evil and, yes, you will feel everything beyond 100%. Don't worry, I'll live long even after to teach you new ways to invent. You'll have your guidance in how to handle it, as did I, somewhat, but it'll mostly fall on your shoulders, little one. Don't worry, we will always be here if you want to vent. I want you to let everything out of your chest and ease your worries, nobody deserves to go through that alone. Midnight thoughts have me thinking childish things, grown up things, to a future I'm blind to see. Always in my head, fantasizing and wondering what may come to be. My powers are beyond the average capacity.

Jealousy

Everyday I try and try to move on. It's like I have bad timing and my emotions are gone. I see your posts and it's always some celebrity you say you admire. It's silly of me as the conversations run drier. Sometimes I feel bad because it's always the ones one wouldn't expect and daily it's like you're falling in love with them and not me. I absolutely hate it and I have to let you be. I've already offered you my heart yet you say you want to marry them immediately. You don't want to date anyone but why them? What is it about them that you see and believe a fantasy from the tabloids? Why are they so special and not me? It's childish but it's never me. I'm always the last one. I hate it. I hate this feeling of jealousy and I can't act on it. I refuse to act on it and I will not do it . I poison myself on the inside seeing how they're the men of your dreams. Why? I get angry throwing tantrums like a kid. I have to keep it under the lid. I'm just as successful as they are, I'm deeper than them because all you see is just the surface. Still waters run deep and that's me. Maybe it's not. Maybe I've finally cracked. It's not on purpose but you are making me have a bad day and I'm an idiot for letting it happen. Why can't I move you like they do? I want to tear my heart out and hit the reset button. I wish there was a way to click the switch and shut off my emotions. I need to let go. I need to love you a little less or maybe not at all. Maybe it's just that, a fantasy. I still can't help how I feel. I feel dirty and slimy as an electric eel. It's embarrassing, to say the least. I know I'm good enough and better. Still, I can't shake it off.

Sometimes I think you're a blessing. Sometimes you ruin me. All this pain for something that's non existent. Shove it down my face, why don't you? I can't help but continue feeling blue.

Unloved Soul

What motivates me to be mega successful? It's the fact I haven't been loved properly. I always get rejected or feel rejected. Sometimes I don't compare but sometimes I wonder how do I compete? I'm just as rich, just as successful, as any older man that seems to be everyone's type. I'm never anyone's type and they get on board with all the hype. Sometimes it feels like I'm never good enough but I know I am. I will not stoop down and question my worth. Why do you tell me you don't want to be alone with me but you do, deep down inside but couldn't risk it and how you can't say no yet you did to me. Why did you go with him? If nobody loves me, fine, I'll make my own path. I already love myself more and more each day and no matter how much my heart yearns to be loved by another, I don't need them! I will suck back the tears that want to fall down. I don't have anyone to spend time and money on so I'll spend it on assets to make me richer. It's the only way I know how to make myself happier. It's too late if you want me by then. You're superficial and flakey, maybe I'm just bitter. This is why I distance myself from people. Even when I'm busy I make time for you but there's always a delay. Maybe it's me being childish and that's why no one wants to love me. It's fine, I'll let it be. I get it. You'd rather go with a man that continues to hurt you or doesn't exist, that's why they say they're the men of your dreams. I'll be the one that's running for you but you don't want me. You only want my body. I hate that. I don't have to keep proving myself to anyone but my damn self. You see the thundering rain and lightning? That's me. Crying over nothing small yet important to me. Unreciprocated feelings is my torture, a daily struggle, so consistent and constant. Sometimes I hate both you and I for allowing myself to fall in love with you. Perhaps it's not love at all and I never knew what love was because I never had it. I never get what I give back. Sure, there's something waiting for me back there. I'm tired of trying. I'm tired of this feeling. All these emotions that get the better of me. Don't worry. I'll disappear when you need me the most. Where are your fantasy dream men? Go back to the one that hurt you for consolation. Don't look for me.

My back is already turned. Taking hours to respond, that's the thing I hate, feels like you don't want to talk to me. It's okay. It feels like you're just politely responding even when you say I mean a lot to you. It makes me question you. Action speaks louder than words. So ,no, I don't believe you. I have a hard time believing you. It's the same with all of them. It makes me hate them. It's not their fault, is it? Telling me things I don't want to hear but I can't erase it. Sometimes they tell me just what I want to hear with lies through their lips. Sometimes I wish I had better control of my emotions, I don't act on them. I promise I don't, I just write about it. I suppose that is an action. I feel them immensely. It's a terrible trait. I can't bear it. All I can do is go up to the sky and let my rage transform me physically. My hair turns blonde, my eyes go red, my muscles expand largely. I let out wails and cried over people who don't love me back. I roar an animalistic roar. It's always the same as I can remember. Don't feel too bad. I'll be the man and love of my own dreams. I don't need to fulfill the dreams and hopes of others. If I have to be alone then so be it. I don't care anymore. I can't listen to what my heart wants. I have to do what's best for my soul. I won't do this anymore. Nobody ever puts me first. I have to put myself first. I'm always cast aside, pushed away, making room for others. One day that won't be the case. I don't know what it feels like being put first. I don't know what it feels like being a first priority. I don't know what it's like being first on someone's mind. I only know that feeling when I have to do it to myself. I always put others above me and it hurts. The reciprocity is never there. I hate it. I hate them. I hate you. I'm too good for anyone to ever feel like this, to be treated like this. I'm worth more than a thousand suns, worth more than the money in the world. I have the Midas touch. Everything I do, I do it well, I'm talented. I can do anything I set my mind to. Never again. You'll see. You all will see. Maybe. You'll hear from me on the tabloids in the future and wonder what happened to the little innocent sweet boy. I'll tell you. He got tired of being mistreated and taken for granted. I evolved and removed my own kindness. You'll never ever see me again. Go ahead and cry how you always get left. Go ahead and cry how nobody is ever there to help you. Go ahead and cry. It was me. I was there. Don't ever take what I did for granted, you support everyone else but where is my fair share of support? You say you support your friends but you don't support me. I don't get help from you people, only from myself. Maybe a few. Still. It angers me. I don't feel all that helped, I only feel like I'm the one that's always helping others. This is the evil I inherited from my father. I understand him now. Hell, guess I'll join him in his path and be much worse than him. The problem is that he did, in fact, have people that loved him and he always got what he wanted. Every. Single. Time. I do the opposite and I feel as if I'm punished for it. I don't need your pathetic luck. All my struggles have made me who I am, and I am glorious. It made me strong. Even if I turn my heart from gold to cold steel, I'm still 1,000 times better than what they'll ever be. I understand this isn't coming from a healthy place or a good heart, so in the end I am truly sorry. It's a shame I have to have the need to say it, but I'm better than them. I don't need them. I don't care if it's a toxic self help trait. Nobody stepped up to the plate. Nobody proved it to me. What do I know? Nobody gave me the consistency I gave them. I didn't see it. Nobody noticed mine. So why continue now? I'll climb that mountain and destroy the world while I'm at it. I'll make a new one with my own two hands. I'll make beings that'll love me for me, really. Calling me crazy? I can see it in your eyes. No, I don't want to be a god. I just want to be me. I want to be loved. Loving myself should be enough but I've been doing it for so long it doesn't always feel like it is. There will be a time I'll regret this. There will be a time when I have to eat my words. However, until then, I'll challenge anyone to make me think and feel otherwise. I dare someone to try. Fill this gap in my heart, fix me. I'm done trying. People always say they'll be forever alone or wind up not getting married and I've offered that to them and more. Guess I got tired and left, not entirely my fault, is it? I wish it was you to tell me congratulations for my achievements but you just look at them nonchalantly as if I don't mean anything to you. So now I suppose I'll turn my back on everything I have ever loved. Farewell.

Fumes

Poisonous anger. You haunt me as if I'm a toddler. You prey on me and I let you. My heart pumps faster, my chest becomes heavy and my fists clenching like a prized gladiator. I can't escape this, anywhere I go I will feel this forever. I can't even meditate because everything reminds me of things I shouldn't remember. I'm exactly like the lightning in my nightmare, cutting things down in my path. Where is all this coming from, this wrath? I'm trying to break the frowns I'm creating. I'm here, huffing and puffing just hating. I'm such a monster, I don't even need a full moon to transform. When will I learn? I'm facing my demons head on, face to face, all of them only centimeters away from me. What can I say? Hello? You're all me. My blood pressure is rising as I can feel the heat. My sweat becomes cold and I can't tell what it is I'm feeling exactly, mixed emotions I'm trying to defeat. I can pretend for so long. I can't change the tune to this old song. I'm condemning, condescending, alarming and crying. Not with the sadness I have fumed and hissed from my heart. The tears are blood, ulcers in my organs due to anger. This is exactly what I felt when I was younger. What set me off? I spit and cough. The blood I spat on the floor is a disease I created. How do you love a Cancer? You just don't, you find a cure. It doesn't matter how much of a dark horse I appear to be. It doesn't matter how much I channel this anger, putting it to focus towards my goals, I'm still salty. Burn my wounds with acid and salt, make the bloodhounds lick my wounds because their saliva heals all, according to the scientific data. I'm one mistake away from becoming just like them. I point at the men I know of, the men I could be, the man in a child's body, possessed by ancient spirits. Let me take a minute. I need to take control of this. Maybe this disgust stems from a cursed bloodline that has to stop with me. I need to pivot this anger and find an anchor. I know I'm going crazy. It's not the four walls that's making me this way. It's myself and quite frankly I'm a ticking time bomb so I'll have to repel all so I can propel. My explosions are worse than propane. I'm trying to protect those around me because I don't want to be such a pain. I look at the mirror and my eyes, those sad little eyes, I can't even see my pupils, my black irises. Where are they? Punching the mirror, it cracks all around the area of my fist. There is no reset button and forward is the only option, I have to add that to my list. I am a dragon breather, a destroyer with my flames, I have to focus my energy. I have to bend my will to tame the beast that is me. There is something completely wrong with me and I can't seem to stop it. I've already cloned myself because I'm the only therapist I ever need, nobody understands me completely. It doesn't help that I hide the facts behind a smile, truly. The fumes in me is what's killing me, not the cancer. My soft spoken voice, hiding behind that isn't the answer. Stabbing myself in the heart to stop myself, stop the danger and re-emerge like a phoenix years later. I cannot become a traitor, I have to be something greater.

Five in the AM

It's far too hot to sleep with restless thoughts. I tried closing my eyes but my mind went on and on, trying to connect the dots. There's lots. I went to bed at midnight but now it's 5 AM but there's so much I can't seem to stop thinking about them. It's a torture losing sleep and it doesn't help when I count sheep. I think back to the days when I whispered sweet things to your ear. You blushed and giggled, kissing my neck that tickled and you were here. We held hands as tightly as we could, as if something was pulling you. I woke up earlier than you did and it was always breakfast in bed with you. I didn't know how to cook so I snuck out to get the pancakes you loved so much and I woke you up softly with a gentle touch. You smiled first before you opened your eyes and it was the most beautiful thing I have ever seen. You always said I was a little angel born from the moon. You loved saying how I was unique and misunderstood, intuitive and creative. I didn't get why you'd say that but you always had a way with words and I kissed you each time as a reward. You were as grand as a golden globe. I am in my feelings every night, everyday, and I miss you dearly because you're not here with me. You went to heaven before me, too late to see. You were gone at a moment's notice, I couldn't stop it. You turned back to blow me a kiss when you crossed the street, you were taken out so hard something flew out, a car seat. I cried so much and couldn't bring you back to life. It makes me think would this happen if we never met. Should I have held back when I saw you the first time, or would it be something I would deeply regret? The love we shared was worth more than an average Cinderella story, more magical than the little mermaid, more enthralling than sleeping beauty. You saw something in me I haven't seen in a long time, it felt realer than a movie. I love you but you're gone. I stare at pictures of you until dawn. I study the texture of your hair from my memory, I trace the skin I was privileged to touch, the eyes that let me see what you're feeling. Now I'm here staring at the ceiling. Tossing and turning due to what I'm feeling. I replay the videos of special moments to hear your voice because I always call your phone constantly but it's out of service. You loved making me nervous. For my birthday, I remember you sang to me sweetly and softly, a beautiful metronome. You always felt like home. It doesn't matter where we were, as long as you were there. Not sure where to go from here, wish you were next to me but I have to steer clear. I have to get out of here, move away from memories. I'll always visit your grave many times a year. I love you and please take care. I know that somehow you're in a better place. My love goes eternally to you.

Emotional Growth

Sometimes my sense of overreacting is something much worse to the average eye. I did not lie. I'm no hero and when I feel immensely, the emotions are heightened exponentially. It's hard to wrap your head around it but I try. Trying to do better is a cliche. Learning from past mistakes and taking action has to make my own day. There are dark days when we fall but after the storm passes, we have to rise again. Wiping the tears off is what I have to do. I can no longer be blue for now. The silence is what's after me, insanity looming over me. I apologize again, over and over, acting up and I have to take responsibility. I must find the calm in serenity. Overreacting and being dramatic cannot be me anymore. I must look for more. The reason for the misbehavior isn't the lack of self respect, it's that I place all the blame on you when I know I have blame to bear as well. I know I am out of my mind but I'm trying to grasp that. I'm trying to put myself back on earth, I must find my hat. I have to cherish what I do have and take it one step at a time. What I'm doing is a crime. I dislike playing the victim in a fit of rage, I'm also the criminal. I have to face it even if it's subliminal. I have to take a hiatus and dwell outside of my comfort zone and evolve. Maybe the emotional reactions will always be a part of me and even though I do master them, there's much to learn.

Memories of August

18 days into august, ten months since I've heard from you. Six words I never thought I'd see: to be honest, I missed you. You showed me a picture of an outfit you were in and I told you that you looked beautiful. I was truly caught off guard as it was the last thing I had expected, something questionable. I wondered during all that time if you hated me or not while you thought the same thing. I'm not going to lie, when I saw the notification my heart jumped, I felt my body shake and felt a tingling. I was just minding my business when I saw the message. You told me you know we haven't spoken in forever and how you understood if I didn't

want to speak to you, my head spinning in strange percentages. In that time there were a million things running through my head. What do I do? My thumbs were reacting quickly, responding back as I held back what I put myself into. I worked hard to stop my heart from fluttering. We went on as if nothing happened, then some days we would talk about what happened to clear the air with tears of regret and sorrow with some time to borrow. It was a sweet beginning with strawberries and chocolates, making something stronger and newer. With a little alcohol you summoned up the courage to reach out to me, hoping to hell I didn't hate you while I made my peace with your absence. I was already angry that my wish didn't come true and ripped up my note I had tucked under my pillow. Apparently it came true some months after the New Year. Things were simpler then but it's okay, everyone has their struggles. Memories of August when I was caught off guard, never expecting something like this and now I just sit in the dark holding on to the good things.

Little Cobra

A little snake crawling through the grass. The other animals try to check up on him but he's tired of slithering through the glass. When the creatures open up on him and when he opens his mouth, they remain quiet. They don't talk back or if they try to speak to the snake, they act uninterested when they say they care and it feels biased. He has to shed his skin and become stronger because this feels like a bad diet. The little snake sees all but knows not to trust. They pretend to care and worry but they're just being polite and so he
combusts. It sucks because a connection is a must. He's been depraved from the basic decency of such and gets angry, really angry and bitter to the point where he bites and poisons other creatures on purpose. He hates how the other creatures of the forest become close with him only to become distant time and time again, tired of it being wordless. He's tired of feeling alone, being alone, the isolation drives the snake mad. He's dazed because he's been dehydrated but not from water, from being led on to false friendships and romance, always being left while they give the attention he wanted to others. What makes it worse is that this little snake is no average snake, he's a cobra, a king cobra, in fact, while the other little creatures waste their time on animals too weak to even rule the jungle

kingdom. A lion that appears to be strong but is crippled, weak and lacks wisdom. They flock around the magical panther, he lacks intelligence and never has an actual answer. They all said they don't mind hanging out with the snake, talking to him, even telling him he can vent and just express how he feels at any point in time and when he does, he's disregarded and forgotten. The little king cobra knows he deserves better, so he has been plotting. It's sad because he always had dealt with things with the hand he had been given, playing his cards right, but he has been failed more times than he can count. The little king cobra charmed these animals and bit them softly, subtly. They were all becoming dazed. Did the little cobra truly mean anything to them? Now he was left unfazed. As he crawled around, seeing the pile of bodies being dropped, he still felt alone but like the scorpion on the frog's back, he followed his instinct. He did what was natural to him, now he must leave before it all becomes linked.

Discombobulate

Tired of this, tired of how you complain when you look in the mirror, it's me. The haunting feeling of green that doesn't go away, can't you leave me be? I get jealous over things and now you don't even want to talk to me. Always disinterested, hearing all these names I don't want to remember, always boring to speak to when you used to be there for me. Now it's like you push me away everyday. You share and put words of others but I get no praise, saying you'll do something for me but end up never falling through. It's the little things but what can I expect? You never once called me beautiful, you never once said you loved me, all this rage I'm trying to hide yet I detect. The negativity is all consuming but builds on and on because you did walk out on me and when I needed you most, you just bailed. It's both you and I that I failed. I can't blame you for not wanting to support me, the awful things I printed on this page. Still, everything I felt for you there is always a pattern you do which you taint. It's the actions, what you said and what you didn't say. You always say how you'll end up alone but I wanted to be there, be the one, but when you told me you didn't want anyone, I understood but deep down I turned grey. When I see the billboard ads of you wanting someone else that's not me, I can't control it and see red. I told myself it'll be better but deep down I feel hatred not because you don't love me but how it's difficult for me to let go of you entirely because right now you're not good for me. I am a gold bar that cannot be appreciated by a blind person while out there, others can see the sea. I don't want to burden anyone with my faults so I have to deal with it. They say men push down the emotions and don't openly express them but I feel them deeper than any men or women I have ever met. It gets tiring when I still hold on, involuntarily, it never goes away when I try to move on but I get pushed back to you as soon as I'm feeling better. I hate it the most when you express affections towards me and as time goes on you push me away. Tomorrow is your birthday. I feel like we won't talk today and that's okay. Maybe I'll drop by one of the most emotional gifts you'll ever get, unless it gets trumped by some of your favorite things and my gift will be forgotten. In any case, if I ever do leave, it's because I got tired of always being the one to tend the garden while you enjoy the fruits of it and never cherishing what you have.

Push

There's a sad little quote saying if I ever needed you and you weren't there, I won't ever need you again. I need to abstain. Another toxic and uplifting post I see on the wall that says,"I can't force you to appreciate me but you're going to feel it when I'm gone." I'm done. Maybe you'll prove yourself again but for now I'm sorry but I'm done. I hope you remember what I remember, when you were the one chasing behind a loser who constantly ignored you and you cried and wailed. You didn't want to give up on what you felt was important and how everyone does it to you but you fail to realize you do it to me all the time. I'm not saying this to throw it in your face, I just want you to know you also commit the same crime. You can't hold a double standard when you don't want something done to you yet you've done it to others. You've done a number on me, my mind always wonders. You always do those things to me. Where would I be if I rejected you coming back to me? Would I still be at peace or will someone else cause me the pain you do? Better you than me, right? The devil you know versus the devil you don't. Maybe I would have no problem cutting those people out if they reminded me an ounce of you, of how much I thought I loved you, maybe I won't. For all the good and wrong reasons, I still love you but I love others as well. The part that burns the most is they, too, act the same and as distant as you and it's something I always dwell on. It's how I feel, so I always come out of my shell to be forced back in so I can yell. You'll call me disgusting and say how can I love three people at once? It's because I always get left behind the dust, can't ever get past to a certain point and left behind, always feeling like a dunce. Everyone seems to do it to me and I don't learn. I'll come back from this downturn. Always leading me on, pretending they like me to just drop me like a brick of cement. I'm the one that has to pick up the pieces they always flat out ignore, even if I come back stronger there is always a dent.

Chip on my Shoulder

A lone soldier walks the unknown lands. You can see his long strands. He has lived a hard life and been through so much, questioning his morals. He learned he can't beg anyone to stay because they always leave him and he must be stronger than the mortals. He can't beg anyone to speak to him because he's opened up enough, people chime in and give a small ounce of positive attention just to pull back. Most important of all, he cannot beg for anyone's attention because he was always on the receiving end of the short stick and he concluded people are usually whack. It's a constant battle with personality traits not everyone shares. He dropped his gear after a few too many tours, a few too many bullet wounds, his body didn't work so well anymore and it had to be boosted with technology that makes him artificial. His limbs look normal but are unnaturally strong, his heart heavy and broken, tired of seeing all the superficial. The seven deadly traits that make living difficult but he manages; overthinking, getting attached too quickly and easily, over self critical, takes long letting go, sensitive to details, putting others first and moodiness. He's been let down and disappointed way too many times, repeating this event over the course of what I have seen and recorded is a relatable trait. The little soldier looks young but is truly old, tired eyes and a small smile to excuse himself from being late. He fought for what he believed and almost died, as he saw others die, for the cause, for war, for love, for hate. Going back to civilian life was hard. He got tired of investing in people, listening to them, learning from them, trying to see them win, supporting them in all ways possible and falling in love with them each and every day but they never reciprocate ever. They were never his to lose but he lost them all the same whatsoever. He arrives at the little hut and takes his seat. A cup of warm tea with barbecue ribs, he's been hungry for days but continued on. He spoke their language, told them emotionally striking stories, sharing tears and laughs. They've asked him what wonderful person he knows was born in June and he immediately thought of her but just said, "me." They gave him a blessed necklace for their gods, their spirits, their beliefs and he put it on. One tear falls dramatically down his cheek, remembering telling a girl he used to know that no matter how complicated things got he still wanted her. All for what? A believer, maybe an amateur. He wants the purest form of love, missing out on being kissed while he was asleep while he's done it for countless others. Then he remembers about war and told these people what he went through, how he lost his brothers and sisters. He tries to pull himself together but the little guy just breaks down, angry, alone, sad, emotional. A chip on his shoulder, poor little soldier. He thanks them for his time and goes to sleep, to get up early to continue his journey to a path not even he knows will lead him, with no specific destination.

Stop Forgetting about Him

Curly haired, somewhat good natured boy but tired. He might have a savior complex but he's accustomed to helping people as they reach out for him even if he's a little liar. Sometimes they just don't check up on him and it hurts because he always cares for them. I promise you he doesn't want a gold medal or a star next to his name on a piece of paper, all he wants is reciprocity. It's hard for him to even date although he's always up for a challenge, struggling through his own complexes to make the other person happy. These days, according to his observations, everyone is stuck on an ex or broken from something they can't let go. Sure, he is insecure at times and a high maintenance on his emotional rollercoaster issues, but no. When you're truly good you don't expect anything from anyone you ever gave to. Maybe he's not so good. He needs to feed his soul with love food. He's always trying to fight it off but he's always in a bad mood. He's always sending paragraphs that shows his deep emotions to people he cares about but what response would he get? Short sentences that basically say nothing, something that can easily be won in a bet. He's getting tempted everyday to join the dark side, he's been down a long road and has already been tried. His attitude and his pride. It's all being tested time and time again and is trying to go with the tide. The current is too strong for him and doesn't know if things are pushing him in the right direction. Correction. There is always a conflict but if he's led astray, there will be no conflict. It will be too late for him now. He was supposed to be the good one. There might be something off about this curly haired boy and I definitely don't want to find out, so I advise you to run. He didn't ask for much, maybe he did. He tries to keep everything under the lid. He doesn't want to be worshipped, he just wants to be loved back. He doesn't know how to identify what's wrong with people by the surface, just helping them on the inside. The people he thought he was close to usually distance themselves from him and he doesn't know why, emotions running deep in still waters. On the surface he's like you and I, funny, moody, can articulate who's ideas intelligently. Him being temperamental is on the surface as he remembers he was dedicated to songs to an extent in the past while he dedicated so many, too many. Except now when he hears the song you're beautiful, seeing your face in a crowded place, not knowing what to do because I'll never be with you makes him go crazy because it wasn't for him. It's what he feels yet being overlooked without a whim. It's confusing, consuming, overwhelming because he writes to them so beautifully but maybe it's unusually clear he won't be the one and deep down he feels gloomy. It's not like she's the only girl in the world for him, but for the past three years she's all he thought of and fell in love with others but they didn't give him what she did. It is quite unfortunate because everything she gives him she yanks it back, as if you're dangling a carrot in front of the donkey. They say there's three times in life you fall in love but they're wrong, maybe. You see, this boy can't even tell anymore but only walks in life through emotionally. He loves so hard, which can be cliche to most but felt only by a few, truly. It's going to be summer time soon, maybe his birthday will be remembered by everyone except whom he loves and it's okay. One day, as predicted by his beloved tarot reader, he'll be loved and wanted by many, but it never was about quantity but quality. She'll miss him when he's gone, missed him like she did before but this time she'll realize her mistake and even if she ever loves again, it won't be the same as the curly haired boy. The affections will have gaps, knowing she will never find the right one, even the many men of her dreams, it won't ever compare because he's not her type. Even if he's not older, even if he's not anything she believes she ever wanted, he is all she ever needed deep down inside and now all she'll ever do is swipe. He was everything she desired but never knew, liked him back but she didn't know, with her indecisiveness and not knowing what she wanted, he walked away. Perhaps he walked away from all three and from a distance can feel that they are all lonely. Even if he cloned himself to love them all, maybe, it wouldn't be enough as the real curly haired boy. Missing out on something they took for granted, now they will know what they lost. Goodbye, says the boy, in three specialized and personal letters he left. He drove away, never looking back, looking forward to living in the west.

Raven Heart

"Sad again, little boy? Crying again, little boy? Angry again, boy?" I'm in prison again, in a cage where the devil is the correction officer. He reminds me of how I felt, whom I loved, trapped in behind this gate he is my oppressor. He opened it and walked casually ready to torture me. He put a gentle hand on my head and made me think of her. He reminded me of how I felt, how I had to move on, no more hurting. No more waiting. You had your chance and you blew it, but I tried to be understanding. The devil punched me in the gut as he laughed at how it hurt more mentally than physically. He reminded me of how much I loved her smile, her laugh, her body, her colorful bright eyes and how much I loved her entirely. The devil didn't need any guns or knives, he remembered what he needed vividly. Raven heart, capricious, malicious, too close between love and hate. It's way past eight. The devil didn't care. He knew there was still good in the little boy. He wanted to break him again and again, but the boy picked up the pieces. Luckily, he suffered enough to be able to take the beating, even if he was consumed by diseases. The boy remembered taking the girl he loved to the park, enjoying a warm day in a beautiful garden labyrinth with birds chirping, kissing. In reality, the boy was bleeding. Bruises and all he still held on. He was picked up and thrown into a chair, as the devil reminded him of how he couldn't handle it alone anymore, trying to be strong but crumbled because he had no foundation. He never looked back and became a war lord and forced nations into submission. He instigated civil unrest, took down governments and profited off the sick. The devil smiled as the boy cried in anger, taking a lick. A swing and a miss but the devil appreciated the courage. The boy was too angry to fall in love, as love is the answer in a world of hate, a world he created. Imperialism, a vision he had and was driven. Motivated by a lack of what he truly wanted but was burned to pieces like an all consuming rage. The devil left the cage. The job was done. The little boy remembered everything he didn't want, hearing his love talking sweetly just about everyone but him. He couldn't take it anymore as he was a victim of his expectations, believing he was the only one she loved. With the same dark energy, the little boy will summon the rage every mortal feared and this will make the devil cry. The little boy kicked the cage until the dents became little pieces of metal, crumbling before him. He remembered how she told him she didn't want him to fall for her because all the friends she had always wanted more, which contradicted how she fell in love in friendships, how it contradicted how he felt. It contradicted what happened two to three years ago in that time. He ran to the devil as the devil glanced back and caught a fist that shook the ground, hell was not strong enough of a prison for the boy. The devil winced and flinched in pain. The boy was screaming in tears, remembering that she doesn't like him the same, how she loved how he made her feel but can't be with him. He kicked the devil in the gut, landing a dirty hook to his nose, holding a strong headlock and kneeing the devil's face. An imp demon sprayed mace. The mace spray was no match as the blind rage grew and grew. The devil stomped on the boy, cutting through skin and bone. He was badly battered but remembered how the girl said how she cannot say no and easily gets influenced yet when it came to him, she preyed on him when he was alone. He forgot what it felt like when she left him and even though they forgive one another, he was salty for the fact that she used the word "never". The boy kicked and broke a lever. He swung it around, battering the devil's arm like a savage. He still loved her when she told him how she would release all her inhibitions if a certain someone came onto her, making him remember how when they were together for a short period of time, making him feel bad for feeling what he felt. As the batter shattered the bones of the devil, he remembered telling her he didn't like that and she told him she didn't care because he wasn't hers, how they were not together and it hurt more than being whipped with a belt. One arm down, another to go, as the boy destroyed the knees of his enemy just by applying some pressure on it. He stared into space briefly, remembering how she told him how they can run away for the day. How they could male love under the stars and how she never knew she wanted and needed him until she had him. Brushing it off, the boy proceeded to bash the devil's face until he became unrecognisable to the point where it was just a hole, impaling the devil in the brain. The boy screamed to the hellish sky, remembering how she dedicated a few songs to him because one day it hurt her how she hurt him, how she liked him a lot but couldn't be with him, he felt confused and thought it was a lie. He kept kicking the body, remembering how his heart fluttered when he went back to her. He comforted her but maybe it was corrupted. She felt bad for what she did and both promised to never do that again but both were weak, immoral and fell again and again. She left him to rage on his own as his mother died. He took over countries and when she came back to him, hoping he wouldn't hate her, he stopped. Then again and again, kicking and remembering. Continuing. Raging. Cursing.

Emotional ATM

My love and hate are confused, morphed into one because I am too petty to see. I try my best not to judge what I see yet I do, but people trust me with their secrets and feelings. I consol them, I coddle them, I hug them and always know just what to say because I'm the one that's healing. I always feel better when I'm doing the helping but it's rare to find someone who can do that for me like how I do. I was told when people come to me for help, I'm always there but when I want it, I get judged before finishing my story or just get ignored completely, leaving conversations unfinished. It's a confusing time to be in, as I get told I'm distant yet I always respond to get ignored or for them to always be leaving. It's ironic, the treatment, it's almost iconic. It's almost as if they want me to be a villain but maybe it's because I want to think I'm never wrong. With all the money in the world I still feel like I don't belong. People can deposit their feelings into me and withdraw the little positivity I have left. It's okay, I've asked for it, I've welcomed it. It's not a race and I won't be taken out. It's supposed to build character but I'm not sure if this is even emotional abuse and how much I can take. I just trace my finger on the water from the lake. I make little heart shapes and remind myself for being dramatic. Sometimes I wonder if I am acting erratic and if I'm a lunatic. I think it's all the stories I heard, all the events, everything that was made personal because they were all a secret narrative. Maybe in hindsight I was too young and I was traumatized, or maybe people avoid me because I'm talkative. Not sure, perhaps I need a laxative. A metaphorical one to ease out the emotions running through as I figure out what's wrong with me. What do I fail to see? How can I be this way? They say how time is a valuable asset, how money can be recovered but not time, as people rob me of mine. I love to help because I probably feel like it's what people love about me, an emotional ATM, but I can't help but notice I can't get the same thing from them. I feel like I am driven by insanity, it's something that escaped and skipped through my fingers as I tried to help humanity. Maybe I already am the villain, telling a sob story. Everyone has one, it's normal, and I am in sympathy. Maybe you'll be the judge of that, as everything around me is in flames but I'm too blind to see. The monster above me is facing me, staring at me, looking at me as he hangs above upside down with a frown. He's actually right side up with a large grin, a stupid smile, loving each moment I feel hurt as if he had something to gain.

Teacher

Waking through the halls, people around me believe I'm a new student. I walk around, head held high with amusement. Other people I work with think I'm a child but I'm smarter than your average. Boyish charm, curly hair, smiling as if I was a young one, drinking a cold beverage. I play around and hug the kids, always affectionate and they've changed me. I'm always better, in a way, when I'm with them. They saved me. Then I saw you. I like her face but I fall in love with her personality. You told me you were looking for me as it went over my head, arms extended out which may have meant you wanted a hug. I smiled at you and just shrugged. I always catch you, I always just sit there and admire you, my eyes just tracing every part of you. Sometimes I look like I'm not in the mood, huffing and puffing but I'm not really mad. It's just my resting mean face because I don't smile much, don't have much reason to unless I'm being fake. You pulled the brakes on me. When I look at you, sometimes I'm just feeling soft and high. I laugh with the kids, well, they give me a genuine reason to smile, guess sometimes I'm very shy. Taking off my jacket one morning, you told me you chased after me and ran outside to return something I've dropped and I hope it wasn't a lie. I said that was the most adorable thing I ever heard and smiled at you, thanking you, checking you out subtly. I always keep my head down, relaxing, chilling and sometimes you would come about, extending the vowels in my name in your sexy voice that immobilizes me. Sometimes my stern looking face makes me look older than I am but my body makes me look like I'm sixteen. I love it when you look at me and smile. I love it when I stay and help for a while. I love it when it feels as though you care about me, asking me if I ate already or if I'm here to stay. When I gave you the little gift, I wish I had a perfect recall because all I remember is you being excited like a girl getting something she always wanted on her birthday. Some of the kids love having me around, hugging me and calling me a father figure, sometimes I wonder about that and make me pensive, having a lot to consider. Teacher. One lady calls me "teach" and loves how kind I am because I try to be. She doesn't really know me. That's okay, she's a sweet lady and helps as much as she can. I have to do the same, walking in these hallways as if I'm one of them while I do act and talk like them, nearly all of them having a larger arm span. It's an exciting little place, a lot of going on, even some headaches, but there's love in between the halls, love I send from me to you. The little slim lady, I'm sure you have a clue. Until then, I'll be seeing you hopefully in September when the weather is better, when times are better.

Gemini

I always act as if I'm so great but I'm just like the rest of you and sometimes I act like a true Gemini. On the surface nobody really knows me but I am more than meets the eye. I have layers and layers people can try to pry. Everything is a duo thing with me and I'm as confusing as I can be. My face expresses the emotions I have but you can't always tell what I'm thinking while I take a knee. A double life, being a different person around different people. I try and try but I'm not on their first priority but when I move away it's like everyone wants me. I can hold on to the anger and hatred like a cancer boy but then I am also logical and artistic with words like a Gemini. I'm not two faced, exactly. My mindset is multiple as my thoughts race, getting excited. I can't always speak right and stutter, missing the basics of bread of butter. Always talented, somewhat educated, aspiring to learn when I can, moving too fast because my feelings catch up with me and clogs my brain. It goes the same with my heart recently, something I don't know if I can embrace completely. I'll admit for the time being I am in love with three people mainly because no one ever shows any consistency. Every time I try there's always a downturn so I suppose the older I get, I have to brace for impact and keep romancing. I promise even if I was born under the Gemini sun, my true nature will make me a one woman guy. I've never really been shown true loyalty, getting back everything I gave and getting spit in the face. Of course this adds to a dramatic effect but sometimes the exaggeration is how I feel on the inside, wondering if my words and actions make people angry at me, making me a disgrace. It's confusing when people say they'll miss me and how they won't stand losing me, won't be getting over me, but why do they misplace me? They place me in a box in a forgotten corner to win a rat race. It's like I mean nothing and when they win the race, I've been gone, feeding my brain some knowledge from this bookcase. It can get very lonely at the top and always misunderstood, wishing someone would pull me down to a place of care. Gemini Man, more like a boy who's seen his fair share. Crying over little things that don't make sense to you but it does to me while I pull out my hair.

Sun Gazing

Do you hear that? The guitar playing on the G major, speaking to you in a friendly chit chat. Every time I see you, it's like looking at the sun because even when you're gloomy, you're enjoyable to look at. Words cannot express how you make me stutter even when I see a glimpse of your tat. I don't know why or how, but you and I are mirroring each other like a copycat. Allowing me to call you on a first name basis makes me feel like I'm floating on an oasis. It feels unreal to me, almost weird, because to me I've put you in this jar where it's like you're forbidden, hidden, with a lot of respect but now it's been given emphasis. Again at your good graces, we play and dance along playing with fire, taking chances. I wonder if this feeling is infectious because I'm lowering your guard down, I'm tearing down your walls, slowly and easing up to you, warming up to you, now I know we'll be going to places. When we are in the same room, they see our bright faces. Sometimes I am speechless and try to hide my flushing red cheeks, blushing like an idiot but I have to hide it before I seem suspicious. With little effort on my part, casually walking by with ease, solving problems as if I had the answers in the back of my hand, you praise my greatness. My childish grin says it all while I'm trying to hide myself from being flirtatious. You make me drop down my guard, too, making me come out of my shell when you smile at me. I lose myself, floating in the air as if there was no gravity. I can't find the roots to this tree. I feel at ease and my heart flutters and grows wings on its own, being feathery. Sometimes it's strange how I see things, sometimes you're indirectly spoiling me, always acting so sweet, making me melt and drip like honey. I can't disagree that you are the key. You unlock all the things I am, all the things I see. The things I see in you is like a reflection from the water staring back at me, could this be a reality? Your skin is bronze, always looking healthy that radiates like a golden bar, feeding off the sweet, juicy vitamin D. Sometimes I get so nervous I crash into a wall, bumping into the door, making me go on a silly spree. Sometimes you act like such a responsible adult, sometimes you act like a child, so carefree. When you get angry you would scream like a banshee. Sometimes it would make me jump and that would make you laugh at me, softening your tone and being delicate like a rubber ducky. My heart sank the day you left early but it did a whole 360, 720 backflip when you told me I was your trustee. Who would've thought that would be me? It'll take some getting used to calling you by your first name but I'll love how the vowels will connect on my tongue. You make me feel young. Sometimes I can say the stupidest thing and you'd be laughing way too hard, harder than you should, needing to catch your breath as if you needed a new lung. I got chills and goosebumps when I heard you sing that song. My legs grew weak as you sang that song. You make my head sometimes when you're there and when you're absent it's like I was strung along like a string.

Fast Paced

It's like a race, seducing her with words to go way past second base. Is she ready for the sweet, long embrace? We close up what's between us, the space. Angles are everything when you tilt your head back, looking at me longingly with that face. I don't know if I can keep up with that pace. Pushing and pulling me like the wanes and waxes of the moon, I know we both are a mental case. If I went to another place, being so far from you, it would be hard to replace. I would sit in my chair, ruffling my hair in disgrace. I would regret it so much and wish to take it all back to the day I caught you off guard as you felt weak in the knees as I tied your shoelace. When I looked up at you to see that secret, seductive grin, you impacted me to my core, accelerating the prophase. Every cell in my body screamed that I wanted to kiss you before I got yanked away just in case. When you're sad and frustrated, tired and alone, I'll say "hey" to check up on you, to see if you're okay. I'll make your day. I'll fill your glass with some Chardanny. I'll be your lending ear, paying attention to everything you have to say. Take my hand and we can make this pain go away. Let's hop in your car and ride down the freeway. We can enjoy the mental foreplay. I can tickle your thoughts and keep you company on a Friday. I can spoil you and make a whole day out of it, I'll take you to see your favorite screenplay. You said you can't even take care of yourself but I promise I'm here to stay. I can make things run smoothly, help organize things in your life so you can actually have time to enjoy a sundae. I don't mind this little delay. I'm patient enough to play the long game, pushing and keeping the twisting thoughts at bay. You're special to me that I'll mark a day on the calendar, to celebrate you, making a holiday.

Bad Wolf

I can't remember what it was I did, crash landed I did to the spaceship. I landed on an unknown planet, causing a giga explosion which I'm sure appeared on someone's radar, a big blip. Everyone I killed on board for a mission I had to take based on a coin flip. Do you see me from up there, red siren or are you going to punish me with your whip? A soldier of fortune enhanced with cybernetics, I had to get a grip on this trip. Soldiers already taking aim at me, with their rifles and laser sights ready to empty the clip. Unarmed but dangerous, I observed what was going on and took advantage of the dip. With my enhanced speed and unequivocal timing, I broke a few knee caps, tore some collar bones, broke some shoulders and disarmed them with the help of what's inside me, a microchip. Taking a lay of the land I infiltrated their vehicles and drove to their leader on a hoverbike. It was no easy task as my heart spiked. Going about this like a warrior, all warlike. This has to be the last thing I have to succeed doing before I die, should I die, so I can fall into deep sleep, all dreamlike. On this Oppressor Mark II, I was able to aim the missiles at the enemy with each precision launched strike. I jumped out of the hoverbike when I reached his castle. The drones and tanks are after me but I ignore them, with this one goal in mind, I am the lord and the vassal. The ogre king stood up, armored up with liquid metal that was almost impenetrable. Wasting no time on a villainous speech, he powered up his power spear that can cut and slice through anything and I know this won't be facile. I was unarmed but I broke the closest thing near me to use as a weapon, the head of his statue. It was too much of a hassle. He pierced through my bones and skin but I was going to dethrone him in front of the council. It seemed like it was hopeless but I remember everything I needed to fight for, everyone I failed to love properly and smashed the statue head at his jaw. This gave an opening to go against the law. He was dazed and confused as I took his knife from his ankle and sliced through as quick as I could and they all saw. From a distance, in the terror and agony, I summoned the last remaining strength to insert the blade in this ogre as his suit powered down. Now he was a lifeless body that turned to stone as I let out a brief hurrah. I collapsed, victorious and battered with a conscious I know will gnaw at me.

The Empire of Bones and Smoke

Welcome to Hell, welcome to those that have touched the bell. Have you been well? How long will he sit there and dwell? He escaped hell to climb his way out of a hole, with everything he did to get out of being under the spell. The sky is red, helicopters swerving, searchlights looking and looking but find nothing to see or tell. The boy crawls from out of the sewer to see the rage in their eyes. They know the truth from all his lies. Sniff, sniff, he can smell the fire and smoke, all getting larger in size. From the distance you can see millions of people walking up the stairs fighting to be the king of the hill, to obtain the holy prize. The man who is the king of the hill fought for his life, his throne, his power, his family as he easily takes down his foes. The boy froze. He was in shock at how the king was victorious each and every time, the king of an empire of bones and smoke. The dead do not Rest In Peace, everything is a joke. Every single person in this city is out of their minds, high on coke. Some even begin to choke. A scary old lady in a cloaked hood drenched with dry blood says the boy is to blame, the boy was the prince but was murdered before he woke. There was no evidence of the killer and no reason to provoke. The king on the hill went mad and he attacked everyone to find the answers he could not find from the ancient tree of oak. The king was a celestial being who brought peace, harmony, love, and prosperity. He gave the people a vision but without his son as his right hand, at his side, he cried in pain as he took away the lives he swore to protect but now lacked clarity. "Father! No! I am alive, can't you see? Please stop this madness and stop this insanity!" For all the quick dexterity, vulgarity the old king thought he was hallucinating vividly. This angered him more as he used his actual angelic power to wipe out the forces that opposed him swiftly. The boy forced wings to grow from his back and flew to his father's side to stop this evil and wicked war waged by one man that took down the empire severely. The king attacked the boy thinking it was a trick. The heat of the moment, the poisonous anger the boy fought back. They were equally as strong and quick. Trading blow for blow something clicked. The boy was the kind and the king was the boy but the realization was interrupted by a kick. "Why do you do this? We are one and the same and I'm homesick." The king is in tears because he has been playing too many tricks and wouldn't even trust this to poke 6 feet away with a yardstick. A most literal representation of internal conflict so much so that it's sharper than an ice pick. Both of them fighting with a strong conviction with a forgotten reason as to why, something that'll contradict. Observing from afar I can see the people have had enough but we're powerless to stop the prince and the king. It doesn't matter which one is evil and which one is good, I simply cannot watch and predict. They might be other versions of myself but this cannot go on and I must be strict. I unleashed an unholy beam, a light too bright that'll blind you even with a little glimpse that'll leave a strong burn. When will I ever learn? I had to fix this, undo this but even then when I destroyed them all, the prince and the king were still fighting. Each one not budging an inch, an internal conflict manifested to see how I will turn out years down the road.

The Land of Dreams and Snow

I didn't know this existed, getting off the ferry as the cold wind blew on my face. My parka keeps me warm in this strange, new place. The snow is fresh and feels different, as the flowers from the trees are pink, falling on the ground as if it were a race. It's a beautiful country out here, a whole different universe. I can feel it lifting from my soul, the curse. It's like a twilight, a mixture of an odd spring and a cold, blue winter. This place is beyond its time, bright colors that shine even if it gets dimmer. It's a mystical feeling I get, even though I'm cold, shivering with excitement, I can feel my heart cry out. Maybe this start can remove my doubt. This is the land I've heard so much about, the land of dreams and snow. Everything is so clear here, everything just goes with its synthetic flow. With my long hair covering my eyes, I accidently bumped into a beautiful woman I sensed familiarity with. I apologized to her as I moved the hair from my eyes and thought she was a myth. Her chinky hazel eyes that changed color under the light. Her prominent brows were symmetrical, beautifully arched that took away my might. Her nose was as if it was painted by Michelangelo and I just wanted to place my lips on it, giving a gentle kiss. Her lips were magical, full, colored with dark red lipstick which made me stare deep into the abyss. I saw them move in slow motion but I didn't hear anything, as my face turned bright red as I moved my eyes to her long and thick wavy hair that made my mouth tremble. I needed to reassemble. "You've been staring at me for quite a while now. Do we know each other?" It took me long to recover because I was admiring her color. Her aura was strong, energetic and determined. "It feels like I've known you from somewhere but it's as though I was missing from your life and you from mine, an extraordinary person." She flickered a smile as I studied her, her strong shoulders that looked perfectly formed and able to carry lumber. I'm sure she's embarrassed and self conscious of it but I wouldn't know, I just know I absolutely love how her hips look, strong and sensual that is doing a number on me. I blurted out if she wanted to go on a little adventure with me and I was surprised she said yes. I planted a quick peck on her cheeks and it felt warm, lively, but I had to suppress. She grabbed me by the hand and we ran to the nearest shops with bright lights. We ate extravagant food and sipped on some wine, renting out a boat to visit a little island. This girl is definitely a keeper, a diamond. She took out her little camera and snapped a few photos of the scenery and when I glanced away looking dramatic and serious, she snapped a few of those when I was pensive and distracted. She laughed at me as we did another tour back into the city, feeling very attracted to her and impacted. She called for a taxi and led me up to her warm and cozy apartment. She sat me down and told me to relax and took out a little compartment. It was a golden pen and a book, she told me to take notes. She actually cooked for me and told me it was a gift, as a way of saying thank you for renting out the little boats. She told me she felt free, without having anyone to judge her and savored the time we spent. She sat there, waiting to see my expression as I took the first bite to see how much I loved it so she could see what it meant. I was already knocked off by her sweet scent, now she's got me by the palm of her hands. It felt like a dream when she took me outside after we ate, slowly dancing randomly as the soft pellets of snow tickled our skin as she tied something around my arm, some bands. She said this symbolizes good luck and blessings, how it will save my soul.

Catching Me Off Guard

Sweet compliments, making me feel good about myself, dominant and competent. My heart catches a cold, you're saying something casual yet bold. My mind shuts down because I don't know what to say because you just made my day. The words that escape your thoughts into your thumbs that reach my screen and make me blush like a young teen. Stupefied, there's a delay in my brain waves as I try to find a response, making me feel crucified. Feeling like a lazy Sunday, talking to you changes my colors on the inside, changing from the usual grey. Sometimes I go on autopilot, mind occupied with other things, always pensive and always quiet. Two distinct people with polarizing personalities, comfortable with each other and able to tell what the other is thinking, dropping formalities. My eyes wander as my mind races, nothing concrete in the spaces. I may not have realized it until now but you bring both excitement and peace, a valuable part of my life that fits perfectly like a puzzle piece. I look up to the dark, night sky and think of you, seeing all the different colors like the Northern Lights in the comfort of my little igloo. The effort you put to make me get out of my shell, checking up on me to see if I'm well, it just makes my heart swell. I believe I told you numerous times I appreciate you but I don't think it's enough so I must make it appear to be grandeur, my way of thanking you eternally because you're a breath of fresh air. Sometimes I don't even have to try at all, just being natural and transparent to make you fall. Every time I look at you I just think "wow!", struggling and stuttering to express how. Always making sure I'm safe and ready to help when I'm in need, it is agreed you'll not watch me bleed. Tending the wounds like a doctor, the good and positive energy you bring is a healthy shocker.

Scorpio Mentality

I'm a water sign and for so long I fantasized about having a unique mind set like a Scorpio. Naturally they can translate the dark energy of the occult, think of every possibility before you even know. I'm emotional and naive despite everything and use my intuition around people. My guard isn't always up and I take people at face value which can be lethal. I can be eating glass and staring into the abyss. You can tell what I'm feeling just by looking at me, but having a mastered pokerface is a bliss. The thing I can appreciate about the Scorpio is that they can sense you from a mile away and think the thoughts before you even had a chance to wake up. It's a chess game they're not even playing as you're drinking from your coffee cup. If mastered right, under pressure they can have the most innovative idea set into motion in a matter of seconds. Most have been hurt and betrayed for so long they have this sixth sense and it takes a mind gifted from the heavens to be able to understand them. Sometimes they don't get mad, they get even. When they interlock their gaze at you, even if it's a lazy eye, it's not just you they are seeing. They can penetrate your mind, they can penetrate your soul and make you believe something you didn't think was possible. The way their mind works is like this: getting it right is possible, getting right twice is improbable and getting it right three times is impossible. What's scary is that there are a few that can make that happen. Mixed with strong, intense emotion, passion, they are the captain. Either you can say how you feel and risk everything or say nothing and let it ruin you, something I learned from them to an extent. My back is torn and bent. Overthinking is a trait I share with them, always on my mind, speaking very little yet I still speak my mind. Death wants to loom over me and to him I say, "ok, fine. I accept. Take my soul but return it." I still have things I need to accomplish. It is selfish. Through all these years I can only observe and take some traits to make it my own but I will never have a Scorpio mentality but I am fine with that, inevitably. That is another cross to bear and I already have several millions to bear, indubitably. Even with the look of a child it is my greatest weapon other than my mind, I am able to catch people off guard as they underestimate me severely. The upper hand is as simple as that, outsmarting them based on every mistake they make. I am an opportunist, sweeping my foes and adversaries off their feet with the grandest surprise ever, proving them wrong every...single...time.

Artemis

In Greek mythology your name is Artemis but in the Roman mythology it's Diana. Meeting you in my younger years was a pleasure, a gift wrapped up by Santa. Different from what I felt, it seemed like you are a reincarnation of Wonder Woman. Dominican and Arabic is a unique mix where it wraps around my brain like a soft cushion. Your long brown hair was worth being in awe at as you were always too busy to do anything. Things kept piling up for you and I eased your mind as best as I could, trying to do everything. Libra energy, charming, seductive, I was wrapped around your finger and you didn't even have to try. You had a tattoo on your right middle finger, the sign of infinity. I'm not sure what lesson you were supposed to be but in such a short time I was head over heels for you and lost sleep. Your jaw dropping personality, maxing it out with how your curvy body was that matched the deliciousness of your brain, wishing I dreamt of you as I was asleep. I can remember vividly how I made you laugh with my edgy humor, wanting to kiss you at least on the cheek as I studied your lips, becoming an avid consumer. We shared some good times walking around the city, befriending each other as you spoiled me, flying over my head as I caught myself staring at you continuously. I wanted to hold you by your small yet thick and strong waist, wished you had a crush on me back, and kiss you like in the movies with shooting stars falling around us. Beautiful beyond measure, it hurt so much to look at you and remembered when I was with you, conversations and waiting for the bus. I remember sitting next to you in the sunset, scooting over to make room for me as we talked the minutes away. I was young but I felt this need to want to commit to you even surpassing marriage and even the attention you gave me made my day. You brought good fortune to those around you as I felt butterflies every time you smiled. I was on fire upon seeing you but I kept my cool, didn't matter anything I did you were worth to be exiled for. The funny stories you shared got me laughing so hard I wondered how bad I had it for you, always ready to go to war. Spoiling me with food, you didn't mind spending money on me or time with me. A Greek goddess of a foreign nationality. It's been years now and from time to time I wonder about you. I still remember the strong voice and the wholehearted laughter. The little hands of yours that were cute to touch but I knew it wasn't me you were after. Always dressing so simple and casual, always making it work for you. Strong cheekbones that outlined a superior genetic makeup with sexy tattoos that all had a story of some sort. Now you're just a vague memory I'm trying to support. I was too late to ever try to be with you, or maybe I was too young to even expose all of my powers to have you in my arms. I'm still unsure what you were supposed to teach me but at least I can say I learned from your traits because I truly did fall for your charms.

Pinky Promise

Staring into your eyes is like staring at the moon accompanied by bright stars. One look from you, that smile that goes from ear to ear heals my scars and I feel like we're superstars. You can grab me by the hand as we dance together. We hum together and drive down south to take a pit stop on a bench and stare into blank space, enjoying the weather. Sacred words we whispered to each other in vague kisses, making a pinky promise. As the light reflects on your skin, so flawless, I'm lost in your calmness. Very few people can bring me peace in a world where my patience is tested constantly, annoyed at many little things that makes me wonder. I can slam my fist and raise my voice when I'm angry but you remind me to not go under. With a little touch on my face I let it go, releasing a soft, weak thunder that relinquishes my hunger. In a world where my own emotions put me in constant danger, you are my heroine, my healer and the one who is my changer. Usually I come out and feel worse when I talk to some people but with you I feel alright. I can trust you deeply because you won me over with a smile so bright. I don't know how or what it is you do but I know life is cruel and you made me forget, you give me the light. It's relaxing that I have bumped into you, entrusting you with my mind, body and soul, promising to fulfill each other's wishes with a sweet pinky promise. I feel silly when you joke around with me, dancing all silly like in your pajamas. You are my sword and shield, I am your ammunition and rifle, complementing each other even if we are opposite sides of the same coin. The path I set for myself was knocked off course but you found me at my most delicate place and let me join. It was all a ploy because I was your mark, I was your toy. You didn't give up on me but I was the evil you must destroy. From your vantage point, the thick bullet of the sniper you blew my heart away.

Chosen One

When I've given up entirely, it's an action that was thought of consciously. They would fail to reach out to me, it is them who don't want to talk to me. Always pushed aside, treated like a child to where I feel as I don't matter anymore. I was led astray to a dead end, another trap door. No way of understanding how to be helped because it is said I was born to heal. As per usual, an imbalance of give and take, self reliance is all i have ever known and this is what I feel. I am the chosen one, to die and be reborn over and over. To be filled with love only to be left alone is how I die , a poisonous exposure. Then when I am truly gone is when they'll feel the absence, reaching out in hopes of finding me like once before. Only this time I will be the one to ignore. The same as always, communicating and spending time with me when they are bored and lonely only to toss me like garbage when you are done and tired. I am the chosen one, strength is in me, I am wired for this and I must do what is required. I will move on, leaving them in tears as I brush away my own. This is tough but this is the true path to my throne. Being used for my generosity and kindness, now I must shield myself in false pretenses of stoicism and aloofness, casting over to the shadows of my past to burn the bridges. It will be vicious but my time to heal is now as I walk through stone and fire to sit on the ridge. I know what time it is, I recognize the pattern, apologizing to me to act the same without change. I will refuse to feel bad for destroying a connection that serves no true purpose, only hindrance, trust me, I need this exchange. I will rise up and dust the ashes off me because there is no conflict. I have to build newer connections, newer bridges, and when it is time to meet the right person for me, something will click. I must stand and believe this with conviction for my own protection. Should I fall back I will be paranoid and cautious but know I am the chosen one.

Amore Mio

I close my eyes and picture you dancing with me, singing to me, kissing me. You appear only in my dreams and in it I'm always on a boat, searching for a sign of you in the sea. You're like a character I invested when I sit and read next to a cup of tea. I open my book and I see you, I look outside the window and see a woman that reminds me of you. I walk outside my door and bump into a lady that appears to be you. She makes sure I'm okay and continues on her journey. I need some fresh air and have to escape so I took a ferry. When I think of you and imagine what you'd look like, I can feel my cheeks blushing. I'd be all cool and cocky, putting on sunglasses and smiling. I'd lean back and ask you if you want anything from the bodega. You'd chuckle and place your hand on my shoulder, saying how it's okay, that you don't want anything and lift my spirits up with just a wink, making me feel like an alpha. Then you'd play an oldie and start dancing, making me feel silly and laugh awkwardly as I kept myself from asking. You'd then grab my hand and make me dance, too, telling me I'm handsome. I'd smile like a child again and your energy matches mine, making me giddy again. When I wake up from my dream you're not there, amore mio, you're just a memory, a fragmentation of my brain. I wake up in this dark apartment alone with birthday cake candles already blown. It had your name on it as my heart bled from being overgrown. I washed my face to wake up and in the mirror I caught a glimpse of you, the girl from my dreams, hugging me from behind and kissing my face. When I turn around you're missing even after all the ghosts I chase. They call me a dreamer, an idealist, living in a fantasy and when I fall down from the bubble it's hard to land on this space. I've got to find my rhythm because I forgot who you were, remembering vaguely to find a code I can trace.